P9-BZF-710

Last Night at the Lobster

ALSO BY STEWART O'NAN

FICTION

The Good Wife

The Night Country

Wish You Were Here

Everyday People

A Prayer for the Dying

A World Away

The Speed Queen

The Names of the Dead

Snow Angels

In the Walled City

NONFICTION

Faithful (with Stephen King)

The Circus Fire

The Vietnam Reader (editor)

On Writers and Writing, by John Gardner (editor)

LAST NIGHT
AT THE LOBSTER

Stewart O'Nan

VIKING

VIKING
Published by the Penguin Group
Penguin Group (USA) Inc., 375 Hudson Street, New York, New York 10014,
U.S.A. • Penguin Group (Canada), 90 Eglinton Avenue East, Suite 700, Toronto, Ontario,
Canada M4P 2Y3 (a division of Pearson Penguin Canada Inc.) • Penguin Books Ltd, 80
Strand, London WC2R 0RL, England • Penguin Ireland, 25 St. Stephen's Green, Dublin 2,
Ireland (a division of Penguin Books Ltd) • Penguin Books Australia Ltd, 250 Camberwell
Road, Camberwell, Victoria 3124, Australia (a division of Pearson Australia Group Pty
Ltd) • Penguin Books India Pvt Ltd, 11 Community Centre, Panchsheel Park, New Delhi
– 110 017, India • Penguin Group (NZ), 67 Apollo Drive, Rosedale, North Shore 0632, New
Zealand (a division of Pearson New Zealand Ltd.) • Penguin Books (South Africa) (Pty)
Ltd, 24 Sturdee Avenue, Rosebank, Johannesburg 2196, South Africa

Penguin Books Ltd, Registered Offices: 80 Strand, London WC2R 0RL, England

First published in 2007 by Viking Penguin, a member of Penguin Group (USA) Inc.

10 9 8 7 6 5 4 3 2 1

Copyright © Stewart O'Nan, 2007
All rights reserved

PUBLISHER'S NOTE
This is a work of fiction. Names, characters, places, and incidents either are the product of
the author's imagination or are used fictitiously, and any resemblance to actual persons, living
or dead, business establishments, events, or locales is entirely coincidental.

ISBN 978-0-670-01827-7

Printed in the United States of America
Designed by Carla Bolte • *Set in Granjon*

Without limiting the rights under copyright reserved above, no part of this publication may
be reproduced, stored in or introduced into a retrieval system, or transmitted, in any form or
by any means (electronic, mechanical, photocopying, recording or otherwise), without the
prior written permission of both the copyright owner and the above publisher of this book.

The scanning, uploading, and distribution of this book via the Internet or via any other means
without the permission of the publisher is illegal and punishable by law. Please purchase only
authorized electronic editions and do not participate in or encourage electronic piracy of
copyrightable materials. Your support of the author's rights is appreciated.

for my brother John

and everyone who works the shifts nobody wants

All the vatos   and their abuelitas
All the vatos   carrying a lunch pail
All the vatos   looking at her photo
All the vatos   sure that no one sees them
All the vatos   never in a poem

—Luis Alberto Urrea

Darden Restaurants, Inc., raised its outlook and expects
full year 2005 diluted net earnings per share growth in the
range of 22% to 27%. . . .

—MSN.com

Last Night at the Lobster

HOURS OF OPERATION

Mall traffic on a gray winter's day, stalled. Midmorning and the streetlights are still on, weakly. Scattered flakes drift down like ash, but for now the roads are dry. It's the holidays—a garbage truck stopped at the light has a big wreath wired to its grille, complete with a red velvet bow. The turning lane waits for the green arrow above to blink on, and a line of salted cars takes a left into the mall entrance, splitting as they sniff for parking spots.

One goes on alone across the far vastness of the lot, where a bulldozed mound of old snow towers like a dirty iceberg. A white shitbox of a Buick, the kind a grandmother might leave behind, the driver's-side door missing a strip of molding. The Regal keeps to the designated lane along the edge, stopping at the stop sign, though there's nothing out here but empty spaces, and off in a distant corner, as if anchoring the lot, the Regal's destination, a dark stick-framed box with its own segregated parking and unlit sign facing the highway—a Red Lobster.

The Regal signals for no one's benefit and slips into

the lot like an oceanliner finally reaching harbor, glides by the handicapped spots straddling the front walk, braking before it turns and disappears behind the building, only to emerge a few long seconds later on the other side, way down at the very end, pulling in beside a fenced dumpster as if the driver's trying to hide.

For a minute it sits with the ignition off, snow sifting down on the roof and back window, the heated glass seeming to absorb each crystal as it hits. Inside, framed by the bucket seats, a gold-fringed Puerto Rican flag dangles from the rearview mirror. The driver bends to a flame, then nods back astronautlike against the headrest and exhales. Again, and then once more, as the smoke lingers in a cloud over the backseat.

The man flicks his eyes to the rearview mirror, paranoid. It's too early and he's too old to be getting stoned—easily thirty-five, double-chinned, his skin cocoa, a wiry goatee and sideburns—or maybe it's his tie that makes him look strange as he guides the lighter down to the steel bowl. He could be a broker, or a floor associate from Circuit City taking his coffee break, except the nametag peeking from beneath his unzipped leather jacket features a garnished lobster above his name: MANNY. In his lap, tethered to one belt loop, rests a bristling key ring heavy as a padlock.

More than anyone else, Manny DeLeon belongs here. As general manager it's his responsibility to open, a task he's come to enjoy. While Red Lobster doesn't license franchises, over the years he's come to consider this one his—or did until he received the letter from headquarters. He expected they'd be closed for renovations like the one in Newington, the dark lacquered booths and mock shoreline decor replaced by open floor space and soft aqua pastels, the Coastal Home look promised on the company website. With their half-timbered ceilings and dinged-up fiberglass marlin and shellacked driftwood signs for the restrooms, they were way overdue. Instead, headquarters regretted to inform him, a company study had determined that the New Britain location wasn't meeting expectations and, effective December 20th, would be closing permanently.

Two months ago Manny had forty-four people working for him, twenty of them full-time. Tonight when he locks the doors, all but five will lose their jobs, and one of those five—unfairly, he thinks, since he was their leader—will be himself. Monday the survivors will start at the Olive Garden in Bristol, another fifteen minutes' commute, but better than what's waiting for Jacquie and the rest of them. He's spent the last few weeks polishing letters of recommendation, trying to come up with nice things to say—not hard in some cases, nearly impossible in others.

He could still take Jacquie if she came to him and asked. Not really, but it's a lie he wants to believe, so he repeats it to himself. Maybe it was true a couple of months ago, but not now. Jacquie said herself it was better this way, and, practically, at least, he agreed. After tonight he won't ever see her again. It should be a relief. An ending. Then why does he picture himself begging her at closing to go with him, or does he just need her forgiveness?

He exhales a last time and taps the spent bowl into the ashtray, stows the pipe in the console at his elbow, cracks the window an inch, flips open his cigarettes and lights one, blowing out a curling smoke screen over the dope. He closes his eyes as if he might sleep, then pushes back the cuff of his jacket to check his watch. "All right," he mutters, as if someone's bugging him, then slowly opens the door and rocks himself out, the cigarette clenched in his teeth. Though there's no one around, he's careful to lock the car.

There's no wind, just some overlapping road noise from beyond the neat picket of pine trees, flakes falling softly on the cracked asphalt. As he walks across the lot, a crow takes off from the loading dock like an omen. He stops in midstep and watches it glide for the pines, then keeps going, palming the keys, sorting through them deliberately, the cigarette sticking from a corner of his mouth like a movie wiseguy. When he finds the one he needs, he takes a last hit before ditching the butt in a tall black plastic ashtray shaped like a butter churn beside the back door (noting on the ground several butts from last night he'll have to police later).

Inside it's dark as a mine. He props the door open with a rubber stop, then chops on the lights and waits as the panels hopscotch across the kitchen ceiling. The brushed steel tables shine like mirrors. The brick-colored tile is spotless, mopped by Eddie and Leron last night before closing. Eddie's coming to the Olive Garden; at least Manny's able to take the little guy with him. Leron can always find another job—and Leron drinks, Leron has car problems, while the Easy Street van drops Eddie off and picks him up right on time, rain or shine. And while Manny would never admit this, since they're friends, Eddie, being eager to please, is that much easier to boss around.

Walking along the line, he passes his hand like a magician over the Frialators and the grill to make sure they're off. The ice machine's on and full—good. He crosses to the time clock and punches in before he hangs up his jacket, checks to make sure the safe is secure, then pushes through the swinging door to the dining room.

It's dusk in here, rays of soft light sneaking around the blinds, picking out a glossy tabletop, a brass rail, the sails of a model schooner. By the main wait station, a point-of-sale screen glows, a square of royal blue. He hesitates at the switches, appreciating the dimness. Bottles glint in tiers from the bar back, and from the front of the house comes the filter's hum and water-torture dribble of the live tank. If he never opens, he thinks, they can never close. It's a kid's wish. Whatever happens today, tomorrow the place will be a locked box like the Perkins up the road (and he'll still have to show up in uniform for a few hours and hand out gift cards to the disappointed lunch crowd, as if this was his fault). For the last two months he's been carefully managing down his inventory, so they're low on everything fresh. Corporate will inventory what they can use and send it to Newington—the spoils of war. The rest, like the glass-eyed marlin, they'll have hauled away. Probably gut the place, leave it to the mice and silverfish he's fought to a draw for so long.

Why not just burn it to the ground? Whoever comes in is just going to want to build new anyway.

He pops on the lights for the main room and then the bar. Outside, the paper's waiting on the walk, the news already old. He fetches it and spreads it flat on the host stand for Kendra, slipping the rubber band onto his wrist like a trendy sport bracelet—a habit from childhood, early mornings delivering the *Herald* with his father and then later by himself. The whole place may be disposable, and everyone in it, but you can always find a use for a rubber band.

He leaves the blinds down and retreats to the kitchen, stoking the big coffee urn, the spluttering heart of the house, and listens to it gurgle as he dials the safe's combination. The fake-leather envelope's centered with the zipper facing away from him, and locked, just the way he left it last night. From habit he checks both ways over his shoulders before picking out the key. He's never been tempted, but today the money no longer seems his. Even if no one could blame him, he can't see himself jumping in the Regal and aiming it for Bridgeport and Deena's. And anyway, it's supposed to snow, a nor'easter swirling in off the ocean, three to six inches by midnight. He pictures himself stuck on 95 with all the trucks, the state trooper with his baton of a flashlight peering in his window and saying his name. It's just green ink on paper, and not worth a man's honor, his abuelita would say, but, never having had money, he can't help but think that's what this whole deal is about.

The thing is, there was no warning. Their receipts were okay, not great but better than last year—and this was with all that construction on 9 during the summer. They hadn't even gotten their fall numbers. The last thing he'd received from headquarters was Ty's ten-year pin, then BOOM, like an old building being imploded, all of it falling at once like it was made of sand.

He counts the bills twice, then locks the envelope and the safe again and fills the cash drawer of the POS behind the bar, snapping the spring-loaded holders down like mousetraps. When he's done he washes his hands, scrubbing between his fingers and singing "Happy Birth-day" in his head like a surgeon. Ever since a salmonella outbreak in Tennessee, headquarters has been pushing food-safety awareness, and as with every corporate de-cree, Manny's done his best to lead by example. He's whitewashed graffiti and pushed the heart-healthy menu and taught his crew that every little bite counts, trying to produce a magical dining experience for his customers. He's done everything they asked, yet there must have been something more, something he missed.

Using the new handheld sensor, he checks the tem-perature in the reach-in and the walk-in and the freezer, saving the numbers in the arcade-gunlike device as he goes, a night watchman making the rounds with his time key. He runs down the preshift checklist, ticking off his chores in order, getting the soups going in the double Hobart. The snow will help sell the chowder to all the mall-crawlers, the gumbo not so much. It's going to be psycho out there.

There are exactly four shopping days till Christmas, and he still has no idea what to get Deena. Not some-thing for the baby; they'll have to buy that stuff anyway. She's already warned him she wants something roman-tic, like the necklace he bought Jacquie for their six-month anniversary, except that's too expensive, especially with his future so uncertain. Lately she's been hinting that they should get married—not just for the baby, but for them. When she starts in on it, Manny just shuts down, he's not sure why.

The question hounds him through the stockroom and back around to the front. The live tank is festooned with a single merrily blinking string of colored lights, some mangy gold tinsel and a misfit assortment of ornaments that have survived a dozen off-seasons at the top of the storage closet. He's skimming the surface, watching the logy veterans mounded in the corners and thinking of earrings, when the Easy Street van flits by in slices between the blinds. The driver's a good ten minutes early— probably worried about the snow. Manny leaves the dripping net balanced on the filter and heads for the back so Eddie won't stand there knocking on the door frame the way they've taught him at the group home.

Manny strides to the far end of the bar, dips his hip at the corner, then squares, stutter-steps and shoulders through the swinging door. It should be no surprise that his body has memorized the geometry of the Lobster, but today everything seems alien and remarkable, precious, being almost lost.

He reaches the loading dock, and there's Eddie coming down the van's steps one at a time like a child, his head bent as if one ear is glued to his shoulder. His eyes bulge, magnified by thick Medicare glasses, and he wears a permanent grimace as if every movement is an effort. Because of the way his knees developed, Eddie needs two canes to walk. As he heads for the dock, his legs buckle with every step, making him lurch wildly as if he might fall, his canes busy outriggers, saving him again and again. Not that Manny notes this anymore, it's just Eddie walking. Every couple years Manny has to write an evaluation for the foundation, and each time he writes, "Eddie is the best worker I have." And while that may be sentimental, and in some ways untrue (he considers Roz the star of the floor and Ty the anchor in the kitchen), it's no coincidence that today Eddie is the only person from lunch shift to punch in on time.

"Big Papi," Eddie says.

"El Guapo."

"Know how much it is now? I heard it on the radio."

"How much?"

"Two hundred million."

Manny whistles. "How many tickets you got?"

"I got five already. I'm gonna buy five more if I'm allowed." Behind him, the driver waves, and Manny waves back, freeing him of this responsibility. "How many do you have?"

"Bruh, I don't have money for presents."

"Maybe you could buy me some later."

"Maybe."

Eddie hangs one cane over an arm and grips the rail of the stairs. Manny knows to let him do it himself, and then when he's made the top, shakes his hand—a formality that has nothing to do with this being the last day, except Manny can't help but realize this is the last time they'll go through this ritual. How many others, he wonders. Is it going to be like this all day?

Inside he sets Eddie to work on dusting the front—the blinds and then the woodwork—while he changes the oil in the Frialators and gets them heating. Last day or not, he has to stick to the checklist, and lugs a heavy bucket of dark, stinking sludge outside and across the lot to the grease-only dumpster. A sparrow in a bare tree watches him pour it in, riding a branch as it bobs in the wind. The cold makes him realize he's no longer stoned, that that private part of the day is over, one more last thing.

As he's coming back, thinking of a cigarette, Ty cuts him off with his decked-out Supra, honking, then jerking forward so Manny can't get by. Manny holds up the dripping bucket, threatening to tip it over the long hood, and Ty whips into the spot beside the Regal.

Ty's styling in a black leather jacket like Manny's, but the real deal, not from Men's Warehouse, the shoulders and waist tailored, trim. With his pencil mustache and close-cropped goatee, he looks like Mekhi Phifer on *ER,* the same sly smile.

"Say, chief," he says, peeling off a driving glove to give Manny a soul grip. "What the fuck are we doing here? We're just going to have to close early. It's supposed to snow like two feet."

"Three to six inches."

"They said twelve to eighteen five seconds ago," he says, pointing at his car.

"Yeah, when's the last time they were right?"

The clouds are right down on the mall and the wind is picking up. Why should he care if they close early? He doesn't know, but the idea is disappointing. He already feels strange about walking away from the place, as if there's something he needs to prove here, some job left undone. At the Olive Garden he's starting at assistant manager, and while he knows they couldn't just give him his own place, and the pay's the same, he sees it as a de- motion. Deena's happy that he'll be cutting back on his hours. He should be too.

"I still can't believe this shit," Ty says. "This is the kind of shit the navy used to pull on us. I can't believe I gotta put up with it in real life."

"You don't *have* to," Manny says.

"I do if I want to keep eating."

Ty's run the kitchen since Manny was a green trainee. He came straight from the submarine service, and on the line he projects that buttoned-down, no-slack attitude, keeping things moving and chewing out anyone who falls behind. Of all of them, Ty probably has the best shot at finding a comparable job, but Manny felt he needed to be loyal to him, meaning he was letting go of Derek, who usually handled lunch shift, and Rafael, who sometimes covered weekends. They both understood, they said, and, though it went unsaid, they expected him to understand why they stopped coming in after that. Ty says he doesn't mind the fourteen-hour days as long as he gets paid, but with first the seaters, then the servers and finally the back of the house deserting in bunches, the last few weeks have been hectic, and Ty's been coming in later and later. In a way, they'll both be glad when today's over.

"Who've I got on line?" Ty asks. "And don't say Frito."

"B-Mac, Warren and Rich. And Fredo."

Ty turns around and heads for his car.

"Where you going?" Manny calls.

"Home. I can't run the line with three people."

"Five. And I'll be helping out."

"We can't do Saturday dinner with four people."

"Five—and I thought we'd be closed by then."

"You better hope so, cause I swear I'll kill Frito if I have to correct his shit all night."

"You won't," Manny promises, but just to reel him in. Everything today is going to be a test of loyalty (he's heard of headquarters sending spies to check on inventory, especially the lobsters and liquor), and he needs Ty. He'll do whatever he has to to get them through this and to the Olive Garden.

"Okay," Ty says, "but Rich is baker. I gotta have my boys with me."

"Fredo's on backup, how's that?"

"Just keep him out of the alley and we'll be all right."

Ty trades his expensive leather for a spotless chef's jacket and apron, cranks the radio on the shelf above the sink by the back door (Ludacris, thumping) and sets to work in the walk-in, choosing today's specials from what's marked fresh by the color-coded rotation labels. By process of elimination, he announces, the vegetable's going to be cauliflower, which means whoever's assembling is going to have to do a hell of a job garnishing to give the plates some color.

"White food for white people," Ty says.

"Break out the red peppers," Manny says. "It's Christmas."

The coffee urn is popping, and Manny stands on a chair and scoops regular into one side, decaf into the other. As he's fitting the lids back on, Roz waltzes through on her phone, smoking, though she knows she's not supposed to in the kitchen. She gives him a two-fingered wave with the butt and disappears into the break room.

While there's still an hour till they open, it hasn't escaped Manny that the only crew to show up are the ones he's taking to the Olive Garden with him, as if the others have stayed away to teach him a lesson. With all the problems they've had with staffing, he's been able to offer lots of overtime—a bonus during the holidays—but maybe he underestimated their pride. He's not sure he'd come in (but that's a lie: He'd even be on time).

A couple minutes later, as if to disprove his theory, Leron, of all people, appears, shaking snow off his skully and poking his fade back into shape with his fingers. Sometime between closing Wednesday and now he's picked up a blood-crusted mouse under his left eye. He saunters by Manny, now working on salads at a cutting board, acknowledging him with a soft "All right," and there's no disguising the reek of weed clinging to his army jacket. He punches in and stays in the back hall a long time before coming out in a black do-rag and an apron and reaching for the box of latex gloves.

"Hands," Manny says, jabbing a knife at the sink, and Leron smiles like he almost got away with something, or maybe he thinks Manny's kidding, to still give a shit at this point. It's impossible to tell with Leron. From the day he started he's acted like he doesn't want the job, but here he is, after missing last night and not bothering to call in. Without a word, he takes over chopping lettuce for Manny. He's way faster, yet only his arms and hands move, the rest of him stock-still, mouth closed in a flat line, eyes sleepy and unblinking. Ty said he knew a youngblood in subs like that, ended up killing his wife on liberty and they didn't find her till they were well under way. Ty'd take him his meals in the brig. For months the guy didn't say a word, then one night when Ty was picking up his dinner tray, the guy goes, "The beets were good." Having been lost and irresponsible for a while in his early twenties (how Jacquie would laugh at that), Manny wants to think Leron's troubled but good at heart. He's seen how Leron helps Eddie when clean racks pile up on the ass end of the dishwasher, witnessed him stick a Band-Aid on Eddie's hand when he cut himself on a broken water goblet, all with the same placid face. He imagines Leron's different at home, or with friends— that away from the Lobster he comes to life again.

For now Manny's just glad he's here. They're forty minutes away from opening, and he's got no line and only one server. It's not lost on him that Leron's in, while Warren, who he's taking to the Olive Garden, is more than an hour late.

In front, Eddie's finished dusting and is sitting in a booth, rolling silverware into paper napkins, slowly filling several white buckets, one for each dining room station. Roz is spraying down her section, all elbows and scrawny arms, her Clairol-blond ponytail bobbing as she swabs the tabletops. Despite her girlish barettes, Roz is old enough to be his mother. She's a pro, with black nurses' shoes and calves like a mountain biker—and a lifer, the only one fully vested in Darden's retirement plan. They don't even make the nametag on her uniform anymore; he's tried finding it on eBay. Manny can't ask her to do Jacquie's or Crystal's or Nicolette's booths, so he grabs a squirt bottle of Windex and starts in on them himself.

"What," Roz says, "you bucking for a promotion? Where's your girlfriend anyway?"

"Which one?"

"Everybody laugh," she tells the room at large, and Eddie looks up. "The boss made a funny. I'm sure she'd love it if I told her you said that."

"She'll be here."

"I don't see why. You owe her money or something?"

It's another jab, but Manny can shrug it off. He'll take this shit from Roz because he knows their situation looks ridiculous from the outside, and she doesn't know the whole story. What he owes Jacquie is so much more than simple loyalty. He's failed her in greater ways, things beyond apology. What Jacquie really thinks is a mystery to him. A year ago, she signed the card with his gift "Forever." Now they barely talk. The baby's not the only complication, or Deena, or Jacquie's boyfriend Rodney. All of that's extra, or at least that's what Manny likes to think, separating himself and Jacquie from the rest of the world. From the beginning there was something dreamlike and surreal at the heart of what they had, something unbalanced (anyone could see she was too beautiful for him), but that, like every other serious thought he's had about them, is a guess.

"She'll beat Nicolette in," he predicts.

"You really think she's coming."

"Yeah," he says, then, "Which one?"

"Nicky," Roz says, because Nicolette hates that name.

"She will if she wants her check."

"Now that's lazy, when you can't even get direct deposit."

"I'll tell her that."

"Tell her whatever you want," Roz says. "*I'm* not afraid of her."

And then, as if she can't let him off the hook, she asks, "Who's on the bar?"

"Dom." Dom's a rock, and Roz has always been a little sweet on him, so that's that. Manny finishes Jacquie's tops and moves on to Nicolette's. Roz watches him, shaking her head, then starts in on Crystal's.

"Thanks," Manny says.

"That's my problem," she says. "I'm too nice."

From the front doors comes a rapping on the glass—Kendra, in fuzzy white earmuffs, the wind whipping her dark hair across her face.

"Make her go around," Roz says, but Manny's already made eye contact and set down his squirter. "God, you are such a pushover."

She says it more with resignation than disgust. Kendra is twenty and majoring in business at Central. She swims for them and wears clingy cashmere sweaters and ribbon-thin chokers, a cameo resting against her skin. The guys in the kitchen pay special attention when she zips in to grab a clean rag or more toothpicks. She can render Rich or Warren silent, and while she doesn't invite this kind of worship, the servers can't help but be jealous—it doesn't matter that they make twice what she does. Manny's not taking her to the Olive Garden, so she's doing him a favor coming in today, and he thanks her for it.

"I'd just be sitting around at home," she says, brushing the snow from her shoulders, and he thinks he'll miss her too.

He leaves her to open the host stand and finishes Nicolette's booths, then heads for the kitchen. Ty is scraping the grill, burning off the excess from yesterday, planing it with a straight blade. He has the blower on, the low drone burying the radio so all Manny can hear is a tinny Morse code of cymbals. Rich is in, mixing biscuits, and Fredo, skinny and hunched over, chopping cabbage beside Leron for coleslaw. Their knives clack and chatter against the Kevlar cutting boards.

Rich is okay, he's just a kid, a big shy white boy. He's only been working here since the spring, and he's quiet, so it's hard for Manny to determine exactly what kind of loyalty he has, and what kind of loyalty Manny should have toward him. Fredo isn't as bad as Ty makes out, but he definitely has his problems: Manny still has a fading worm of a scar on his thumb from a hot baking tin Fredo set down without leaving a rag on it. If he could take more than five, Rich might make it. Not Fredo.

The chowder's going, and the gumbo, and the coffee. Eddie turns on the dishwasher, adding another layer of noise. The room fills with a steamy heat, and Manny feels the way he used to in the locker room before a big meet, that same buildup of energy waiting to be released. No one's new here. He doesn't have to tell them they're going to be shorthanded, or what that means.

He goes to the house phone in the narrow aisle by the coatrack and calls Warren's cell, but just gets his voice mail. He tries B-Mac and wonders if they're in this together, knuckleheaded revenge for him not taking both of them.

He realizes he's plucking at his rubber band, snapping it against his wrist, and stops.

Nicolette nearly runs him over coming around the corner. So he's lost that bet too.

"It's bad out there," she says, flinging off her scarf. "A car spun out right in front of our bus."

"Don't worry," Manny says, "I had Roz do your set-ups."

"Unh-uh."

"Nah, I did them."

"Good," she says with a mix of relief and satisfaction. Of all the servers, Nicolette's been there the shortest and has made the most enemies—from the seaters to the bussers to the kitchen. She couldn't have been surprised that he wasn't taking her. Even before he made the announcement, she regularly threatened to quit, once spectacularly, after she chased an old lady who'd swiped her pen, catching her in the parking lot and cursing her out through her closed car window. "I don't need this shit," she said, and threw her nametag across the break room when Manny tried to talk her down. So while he's sorry he has to let her go, secretly he thinks he's granting her wish.

They're twenty minutes away, and Crystal's still missing, and Dom and Jacquie. He expected turnout would be light, but this is a nightmare. He tries Warren and B-Mac again, then rolls up his sleeves and takes over for Rich, working the biscuit dough with his wrists and shrugging when Ty comes over, all pissed off.

"Please tell me this is a joke."

"Don't ask me," Manny says. "Ask your boy Warren."

"I will," Ty says, then a minute later stalks back from the phone and tells Fredo to quit dicing carrots and get on backup. They're good on salads for now. It's time to get the rice going, and the fries.

Manny fills a half dozen tins and fits them in the reach-in. Eddie's just standing around, so he calls him over and makes him baker, showing him how. "You're going to need new gloves."

"Right," Eddie says. "How many should I do?"

"Just keep 'em comin' till I tell you to stop." It's a reckless order, since Eddie's never done it and Ty's sure to need something washed, but Manny's in a hurry and thinks he'll be back to spell him soon enough.

In front, it's so dark out that Roz has turned the house lights on low, giving the place the late-night vibe of a cocktail lounge. Dom's still not in. Manny's got to set up the bar, and asks Roz and Nicolette to slice lemons and limes while he lugs a couple buckets of ice from the machine. The Bombay Sapphire is almost gone, and the Dewar's. As he's restocking the bar back, he catches a car crossing the front windows in the mirror, the misdirection confusing, making him swivel his head to see who it is and then pretend he hasn't, aware that Roz and Nicolette are probably watching him. It's not Jacquie's fast and furious Accord but Dom's boxy gold Grand Am, so he can stop working on the bar and deal with the walk, already covered with a dusting.

The snow's so dry he can do it with a broom. As he sweeps, he casually peers out over the mall lot, crawling with cars, their lights on to combat the gloom and the snow, falling steadily now, straight down. He doesn't have a coat on, and gradually the cold seizes him, stealing his breath, biting at his fingertips, yet he takes his time.

What would it mean if Jacquie doesn't show up? That all his memories of the two of them are untrue, and more shameful than if they'd never happened. Because now he has trouble believing them himself. The day they took off and went to Lake Compounce and rode the rides all day and made out in the Ghost Hunt like they were teenagers. The morning they sat in the waiting room at the doctor's office, not talking. By now these scenes have been stripped of their dialogue and motion. All he can recall are still images—her black hair wet and heavy from the shower, her stockings laid over a chair, the glass of water on the floor by her bed holding the light from the window—yet instead of weakening with time, they've grown more powerful, liable to paralyze him if he dotes on them too long.

Part of him—the responsible, smarter part of him that wants Deena to be limitlessly happy—hopes she doesn't show up. What could he say to her anyway?

Good-bye.

Is that it? They tried that months ago.

He used to marvel at the fact that out of the millions of people in the world they'd somehow found each other, whether it was an accident or destiny or the result of some logical, cascading chain of events. Now, looking out at the snow falling on the darkened cars, he thinks it's an even bigger mystery, and, like the Lobster, a waste.

At least she could have called, he thinks, but even that wouldn't have been enough. What would?

He trades the broom for a bag of ice melter, strewing

the white pebbles like chicken feed, watching them scatter and hop. They crunch underfoot, a different slipperiness, and he thinks it would be fitting if someone fell and broke a hip and sued the company. He hasn't had the snowblower out so far this winter, and in truth is hoping to avoid it. It's always a battle getting that antique started (it waits under a plastic tarp in the dim corner behind the ice machine, probably low on gas). If it keeps up like this the lot will need to be plowed, and he reminds himself to call them when he goes back in. For now, though, he likes being out here alone, salting the walk along the curb, following one wing to the far end where he can watch the mall entrance like an advance scout.

A couple times he thinks he sees her Accord turn in, but with the distance and the cloud cover, every Japanese coupe could be a Honda, every dark color maroon—until the cars come closer and resolve into disappointing Hyundais or Mazdas, cut-rate imitators. On his way back to the middle, he notices the ice melter beginning to work, a tiny circle opening like a bull's-eye around each pellet. It's almost time; even without looking at his watch, he can feel the seconds ticking off like a countdown.

He's covering the other wing, starting at the far end and coming back the other way so he can keep an eye on the light, when a car pauses at the stop sign as if it doesn't know where to go, then keeps coming, following Dom's tracks, and turns in. A big cheaply painted Caprice, probably an old taxi or cop car bought at auction, a real hooptie. He expects it to swing wide and take one of the prime spaces in front, but instead it keeps gliding by as if it's going around the building. He stops salting to watch it pass, standing tall as if he's guarding the place. There are two people in the front seat—a giant black guy driving and, beside him, a tiny brown girl with her hair pulled back and a diamond nose stud. Jacquie.

Being a nice guy, he raises a hand to wave. For a second he believes she's looking right at him, her eyes flashing, asking him not to, and he falters, unsure. He freezes in midgesture, and that quickly they're past him and around the corner, past Dom's Grand Am and Roz's new CRV, dragging a swirling wake of snow, leaving him to contemplate the fresh imprint of their tires. He lowers his hand into the bag and keeps salting as if nothing's happened, sure that behind the blinds everyone is watching.

He's seen pictures of Rodney on her dresser but never in person. He's a cricket player, a sought-after bowler around Hartford and even down in the city. He's been kicked out of a couple semipro leagues because of his temper, and while Manny can take care of himself, it's been a long time since he wrestled, and he concedes that Rodney could probably kick his ass, and that after all that's happened, he probably deserves it. Having wronged him for so long, and so completely, sometimes he pities Rodney even more than he pities himself—until he remembers that Rodney still has Jacquie. From what little she's told him, Manny knows he takes whatever under-the-table jobs he can get because he's not legal, and worries that once Jacquie gets her degree she'll drop him for someone educated. He's asked her to marry him, out of desperation, she thinks. Manny can identify. As humiliated as that half wave made him feel, mostly he was just grateful she showed up. He's okay as long as she's near him, as pathetic as that sounds. In a strange way, he and Rodney are brothers, both of them at her mercy.

The Caprice chugs around the other side, cutting fresh tracks, ass end sliding as it leaves the lot, fishtailing onto the road, then correcting. New York plates—probably not even registered in his name. Not that Manny's ride is any better.

Manny flings handfuls, making sure he's got good coverage. It could save him from having to do it again in a couple hours, or having to fight the snowblower. Jacquie's probably already punched in and hung her coat up (puffy, quilted baby blue, with a white fake-fur collar; when they were together, she thought it was funny to hang hers right beside his, the two pressed together like a clue, though to everyone it must have seemed they were flaunting their happiness). Now she's getting her coffee and pushing through the door of the break room. Now she's checking her section, asking who did her setups.

With all the distractions, he's forgotten Crystal, still

not in, but it's not like Warren and B-Mac in the kitchen. Roz, Jacquie and Nicolette can handle their business. Roz is always bitching about how they need bigger sections to make any real money, so here's their chance.

As he's finishing the crosshatched patch between the handicapped spots, another car turns in, a boat of an Olds with a rust-specked bumper—Mr. Kashynski, Manny's old gym teacher and coach from high school, retired now. He was ancient then, with a chapped ham of a face and a greased-down comb-over. Living twenty more years as a widower hasn't helped. He's a regular, with his own window booth. He'll order the broiled tilapia and a cup of coffee and quietly read the *Herald,* then leave Roz a three-dollar tip. He wheels the big '98 wide and noses into the first spot.

"Hey, Coach." Manny waves, though it's impossible for Mr. Kashynski to hear him through the windshield. Manny digs a finger under his cuff to read his watch (and there's the rubber band again, like a reminder), then holds the same finger up to let Coach know there's still one minute. Mr. K. waves back, dismissive, no rush, and breaks out his paper.

Inside, Nicolette informs him that Crystal isn't in yet, as if he hasn't noticed.

Jacquie's sitting in the break room with Roz, refilling salt and pepper shakers. He breezes through, just long enough to thank her for coming in.

"My car died," she apologizes.

"That's okay," he says. "You made it."

"Good thing too," Roz says. "It's all-you-can-eat shrimp."

"No," Jacquie says, like she can't believe it. "Hell no."

"What am I supposed to do," Manny says. "They've been running the ads all week."

In back, Eddie's still filling tins with biscuit dough, and Manny tells him that's great, that's more than enough, and sends him back to the dishwasher. Rich is mixing tartar sauce. Leron's draining a basket of fries.

"So this is it," Ty asks.

"This is it," Manny says.

"Better pray we don't get slammed."

"Coach is out there already."

"Tilapia," Ty tells Fredo, who hesitates before opening the reach-in, then hesitates again. "White tub, second shelf, right. It's marked right on it."

Manny can see this is going to be an all-day thing, and leaves them to figure it out. (In his confusion, he's entirely forgotten about calling the plow guys.)

From here in it's all checklist. He turns up the house lights, turns on the fake stained-glass lamps over the tables in all four sections. He powers up the sound system and dials the house music to the approved volume, and there's Bonnie Raitt singing "Something to Talk About" for the millionth time. Window by window he gently tugs the cords of the blinds and lets in the gray light of day. On cue, Mr. Kashynski hauls himself out of his car and starts up the walk. Nicolette retreats to the break room. Dom gives him a thumbs-up from the bar. Kendra's ready, hair just brushed, lips painted, a stack of menus waiting on the host stand, two dozen pagers neatly ranked in the cubby behind her in case they get overrun.

"Here we go," Manny says, to himself as much as anyone, and for the very last time he flips the breaker for the neon by the highway, then slides the tab of the plastic CLOSED sign on the front door to the right to let the whole world know they're open for business.

WHICH NOBODY CAN DENY

They come in pairs and threesomes and the rare foursome, mostly wives and young mothers this time of day, escapees from the mall. They come from West Hartford and Farmington and Simsbury and other suburbs Manny's only driven through summers on his way to Barkhamsted Reservoir, and driven carefully, wary of gung-ho cops. Their SUVs chew through the snow and plug the parking spots, for one day justifying their pricey four-wheel drive. They track in clumps of snow, pausing to stomp and read the specials on the chalkboard, then follow Kendra to their booths, sliding in, dumping bags and gloves and jackets, relieved to sit down and gather themselves and compare their loot. They warm their hands over the single cupped tea light, ignoring Manny as he cruises through. They want their waitress. They want their lunches so they can get back out there and get their shopping done.

In the corner, Mr. Kashynski hunches over the splayed-out sports section with his coffee, occasionally picking at his tilapia, his plate pushed to the side. Roz sometimes bitches that he's hogging one of her four-tops, but on slow days she's grateful to have him. Plus he doesn't run her the way the shoppers do, asking for waters all around and more biscuits for the kids, sending her to check with Ty to see if the scallops are frozen or if there's any clam juice in the seafood stuffing.

Manny drops by to say hey, and Mr. K. taps an article with a liver-spotted hand. "We almost lost to Weaver. Weaver! I don't know what's going on over there anymore."

"It's early," Manny says, because he's heard Coach go off like this before. It's the start of the season, and though New Britain's gone through three other coaches since he retired (forced out, rumor was, over a disagreement with someone on the school board), he still gets excited this time of year. "We're still undefeated, right?"

"We haven't faced anyone yet, and we've got less than a month to get ready for Southington."

"I hear they're good," Manny sympathizes, though he's only heard it from Mr. K. himself, and can't remember the details. Like any longtime acquaintances, there's a comfortable slackness to their conversations. Manny can listen to him and scan the room for trouble at the same time, like a cop writing someone a ticket. The foyer's getting busy, with Kendra trying to greet and seat at the same time.

"What's this I hear about you guys closing down? That right?"

Officially Manny can't answer him, but his pause is a tip-off. "Where'd you hear that?"

"Around."

"Not from anyone around here." Meaning Roz.

"It's not a big secret, is it?"

Manny plucks the rubber band and rubs his wrist, stands with hands on hips.

"Damn," Mr. K. says. "I was hoping it wasn't true. When?"

"Tomorrow."

"Jeez, I wish you'da told me. I've got a ton of coupons just sitting around at home."

"You like Italian food?"

He shrugs.

"They should be good at the Olive Garden. That's where they're sending us."

"The one in Bristol?"

"Starting Monday. Come on by, we'll take care of you." Because Manny and the survivors, being new, are scheduled for lunch all week. He hadn't considered it a good thing until now.

"I might do that," Mr. K. says.

"Do," Manny says, and nods to seal the deal, then excuses himself to help Kendra.

One problem the remodel was supposed to solve was

their small foyer. In the summer, customers can take their pagers outside and sit on the benches. Today they're crammed between the live tank and the marlin, blocking the way to the restrooms, and every time the door opens, the wind makes them groan. Kendra's not at the point of taking names yet. There are open tables, she just can't get to everybody at once. When she leaves her post to escort a two-top in, the crowd mutters. A tall bald guy in a khaki trench coat over a suit and a red bow tie bellies up to the host stand. Manny steps in and asks how many are in his party.

"Fourteen," he says, and looks behind himself. "We're not all here yet."

"Do you have a reservation?"

"The girl I talked to said you don't take reservations."

"We don't, but for parties of more than ten we like to have some advance notice."

"That's why I called," the man says. "She made it sound like it wouldn't be a problem."

"It's not," Manny says, nonchalant, thinking it was probably Suzanne and that it was probably intentional, while simultaneously trying to figure out where he's going to put them all—along the back wall, fitting together six freestanding four-tops—and who's going to serve them. It's a two-person job, so Roz, obviously, since Coach will be holding down his corner for a while, and Jacquie, since her section's next to Roz's. By basing his choice on proximity, Manny doesn't have to admit his natural hesitation to give this mob to Nicolette. It's an office party, always demanding, and messy, and at the end they're likely to pool their dollars and scrimp on the tip.

"Thanks a lot," Roz says, helping him muscle the balky tables into place.

Jacquie pitches in, and so their first real moment face-to-face is an awkward dance with a four-top in the middle of the room, with an audience looking on. He wants to talk to her like they used to, curled into each other under the covers, his lips so close to her ear all he had to do was whisper. She'd laugh and push him away and they'd clinch again, trading secrets from when they were little kids, even the few memories he has of his mother.

Jacquie lifts with her fingertips and shuffles sideways with him, adjusting the table after they set it down so the edges are straight, then moves to the next one. Manny follows. Per company policy, she's taken her diamond stud out, and seems defenseless and vulnerable, like his abuelita waking up in the hospital without her glasses. He already asked Jacquie if she wanted to come with them—them, not him—and she's already said no, so how is he supposed to change her mind now? He can see himself begging her and freaking her out—giving her even more reason to put all of their sorry history behind her.

He remembers working beside her like this just this spring, how sharp and rich it was, carrying their secret; it could pop out in a deep kiss back by the coatrack, a tug on his hand out on the loading dock. Now the same silence between them carries a negative charge, and a dull one, as if they've agreed to keep their emotions muffled, or pretend they have none. He keeps forgetting, they've declared a truce. He's supposed to be neutral.

They arrange the chairs, and Manny signals Kendra to send the party in. The guy with the bow tie nods as he passes, one boss to another, as if Manny's done all this for him.

Nicolette brushes by with an empty tray. With the big party taking up so much space, Kendra will have to double-sit her section, and one of her four-tops is a pair of moms with a toddler who stands on the banquette, bouncing up and down and waving his fists, stopping only to crane over the table and sip soda from a straw. He's too big for a high chair, so Manny detours for a table touch and asks the mother if he can bring her a booster seat.

"That would be wonderful," she says.

He makes sure to wipe off the one he takes down from the top of the coatrack, pebbly brown plastic with twin indents for a tiny bottom. At first the boy sits, interested in the novelty and the attention, but by the time Manny loops through the bar to help Dom with the office party's drink order, the kid's standing on the booster seat, even more precarious than before. Again, Manny's thoughts drift to lawsuits, hefty settlements, the lottery-winning dream of a house in the country and never having to work again. A flash of lightning through the room brings him back—someone in the party taking pictures. Maybe a birthday. They're already loud, blasts of laughter that make the other customers glance over, and again he's glad he didn't give them to Nicolette.

Dom drains one bottle of chardonnay and opens another, while Manny spaces the glasses in a daisy pattern on a tray for Jacquie. They've got it covered, so he heads for the kitchen, noticing on the way a lamp in Nicolette's section is burned out. He unscrews the bulb and takes it with him, shaking it near his ear to hear the filament jingle, then fending off the swinging door with his free arm.

The kitchen's in business, sizzling and chinking and clattering, but with so many no-shows it seems empty, and though he knows better, he's afraid they're not ready. Ty's got Leron beside him on the line and Fredo on backup, shuttling to the walk-in. Rich is baker, while Eddie's racking the very first dishes from the early birds' starters.

"How we looking?" Manny asks Ty, who's stockpiling skewers of grilled shrimp in a chafing dish.

"We're out of king crab."

"That's good."

"Maybe for you. I guess we're pushing the shrimp then."

"All-you-can-eat."

Ty gestures with his tongs at Leron pulling a dripping basket from the Frialator. "Tell the ladies they better tie up their sneakers."

In the stockroom Manny finds the right size bulb. He ditches the old one on his way through the break room, passing Jacquie coming the other way with a bus tub.

"I need someone to clear that four-top for me," she says.

"There isn't anyone," he says, and they fly through their separate doors.

The new bulb works—and helps, since it's even gloomier outside, snow flying sideways across the windows, the mall just a shape. Manny stops for a second and watches the cars crawl along the rows as he clears Jacquie's booth. Shouldering the full tub, he catches a disgusted look from Roz. To even things up, he does one of hers next, then one of Nicolette's. It's just that kind of a day when everyone needs to pitch in.

"Damn," Ty says when he comes in with his third tub. "They riding you like My Little Pony. Giddyup!"

And it's true, he's sweating a little—his size catching up with him, plus the tropical climate of the kitchen. He wets a paper towel at the hygiene sink and dabs his forehead.

When he returns, the little kid has abandoned the booster seat and is hanging off his mother's neck like a

possum while she talks with her friend. The mother orders another Sprite for him, which he immediately spills,
the ice sliding across the table, wetting everything, dripping off the side. Manny helps Nicolette slop it up. After
they change the silverware, the mother asks them to re-
place the Sprite at no charge because he'd barely touched
it. The kid's still climbing all over the booth, snapping
crayons in half, tossing gnawed-on oyster crackers. On
her way to the bar, Nicolette smiles with gritted teeth at
Manny.

"I'm going to fucking kill him," she says like a ven-
triloquist.

"Let the mother take care of it."

"I'm going to kill her first."

The office party is a farewell lunch, complete with
presents and speeches. The guest of honor is a pixieish
gray-haired woman wearing bright red lipstick and a
sheer black scarf to cover her neck. One by one her col-
leagues stand and toast her accomplishments. She sits at
the head of the table, her back to the falling snow, hands
clasped with childish delight at each joke and anecdote.
She's retiring, which explains the gag gifts: a rattling
weekly pill reminder full of Tic Tacs (the same pink one
he used to have to help his abuelita open), a pair of chat-
tering wind-up dentures, a jumbo package of Depends.
Manny tries to smile but imagines his own retirement

party. What kind of gifts would Leron and Rich and Nicolette give him? The applause drives him up front, where he checks in with Kendra.

"Doing okay," she says. "It's getting really bad out."

"Hey," he says, "can you do me a favor and take it easy on Nicolette?"

"I'm just following the rotation. If I didn't sit anyone there, she'd bitch about that. She doesn't even have to deal with the big table."

"I know, I know. This isn't for her, this is for me."

"Fine," Kendra says, pissed off now.

The walk's almost entirely white again, and the tracks in the lot are starting to pack down solid. He's angry, but only partly at himself. He shouldn't have to call the plow guys when it's this bad, they should just come.

He uses the phone on the host stand and gets their answering machine, waits while the message plays, studying the muscular curve of the marlin's body, its hinged mouth and tiny teeth disappointing beneath the spear of a beak. Somewhere under the dust and shellac there must have been a real fish once. How long ago? He can almost see it swimming, thrashing in water blue as a swimming pool, the last minutes before it was hauled on board.

The beep beeps.

"This is Manny at Red Lobster. It's twelve thirty-five and I need someone out here now. Thank you."

Kendra sympathizes—or is she criticizing his ineptitude?—shaking her head as he pushes into the vestibule and grabs the bag of ice melter.

"Hey," he says through the open door, "if you have time, could you help clear?"

"If I have time."

"I'll make sure they tip you out on whatever you do."

She laughs, just a puff, as if that will never happen, because it's been a point of contention forever.

Outside, the wind cuts through his thin shirt, lacy flakes catch in his eyelashes. The slushy ghosts of footprints bleed through the new cover. It's noticeably warmer, the snow heavy as wet cake, crystals sticking together as they fall. He should probably break out the snowblower, but for now he sows handfuls of ice melter, a quick fix so no one from lunch ends up breaking a hip. Far across the lot, a big town plow roams the aisles, blade scraping all the way down to asphalt, yellow light wheeling. It peeps as it backs up, then gores forward again, the diesel softened by distance and the veil of snow, almost like fog, obscuring the mall, a dark block with floodlights burning at the corners, like a fort or a prison. He tramps out to the end of one wing where Dom's and Roz's cars sit in exile and works back toward the Lobster, the illusory movement of the colored string through the front doors and the glow from the windows and the candlelit faces of people eating inside all suddenly, surprisingly beautiful to him, as if he's still stoned. He rests for a moment to appreciate the vision and hears, in the hush, at a distance, the frantic whizzing of a car spinning its wheels. In the storm light, the restaurant looks warm and alive and welcoming, a place anyone would want to go. It looks like a painting, and he feels proud, as if this is his work, and in a way it is, except it's over, like him and Jacquie, lost, gone forever. Is that why he loves it so much?

There's still tonight, he thinks.

There's still today. He still has no idea what to get Deena, and thinks that at this point he really should. He better figure out something soon. He knows from all-too-recent experience there's nothing worse than a guilty present.

The bag runs out before he can finish the slot between the handicapped spots, and in good conscience he can't let it slide. He follows his own already-vanishing tracks up the walk and opens the door. A foot into the foyer the heat and noise and background music surround him. The kitchen's even louder with the grill seething, the radio pumping, the dishwasher cycling. "Where's the salsa for this Aztec Chicken?" Ty hollers at Leron as Manny lugs a new bag from the stockroom, passing the ice maker and the snowblower under its dusty cover. "Goddammit, Frito, where's my linguini?"

Fredo's hurrying over, but his sneaker slips on a wet spot and he goes down hard, dropping the pot, which bounces and overturns, dumping the linguini out on the tiles.

Ty jabs his tongs in his direction. "Why are you doing this to me? Just tell me."

"You all right?" Manny asks, and helps Fredo stand.

"This is not fucking working," Ty says.

Roz and Jacquie come flying in for appetizers but they're not all up yet. The kitchen's getting hammered by the retirement party and the all-you-can-eat refills, and the servers are taking the blame.

"Come on, guys," Roz says. "It's a party. I can't serve half the table."

"Try," Ty jokes.

"Hello," Roz says, "I need to serve the guest of honor first?"

They're ahead on biscuits, so Manny pulls Rich off baker and adds him to the end of the line as an extra assembler. They're far enough into lunch that they can let the bus boxes pile up for a little bit and have Eddie give Fredo a hand with prep.

"I need someone to clear 35," Nicolette says.

"You're kidding, right?" Jacquie asks, because the party's running them hard with shotgunned drink orders and Nicolette's down to the kid's booth and a four-top of grandmothers—notoriously cheap but easy.

"Do I look like I'm kidding?"

"Give me ten seconds," Manny says.

On his way outside, he passes Kendra just standing at the host stand, and he senses—and he's sure he's right—that the power struggle here isn't between him and her or Nicolette and Jacquie but between Kendra and Nicolette, a long-standing beef between seater and server he's done his best to referee. It's their last day, so no one's going to flinch, and Manny's not dumb enough to try to get both of them to surrender.

He dashes a few handfuls over the spot, then stalks back in, ditching the bag in the vestibule. He grabs a tub and buses 35, loops through the break room and finds Jacquie at the bar.

"I don't know why she even comes in if she's going to be like that," she says.

"Like what?" Manny says. "That's the way she always is."

"I *know*. That's what I'm saying. Why doesn't she just stay home? She doesn't do anything anyway." When she's angry she talks fast and her island accent comes out, making Manny feel like they're talking intimately. Even if it's wrong, he wants to believe she wouldn't say this to anyone else.

"She's just trying to get to Kendra—"

"She's useless too. They should be helping instead of messing around."

He sees his opportunity, with the two of them here and Dom busy mixing Lobsteritas, the messy Weather

Channel map morphing above the POS. He hesitates, knowing how easily she can read him. It's not going to come across as casual, whenever he does it.

"Why'd you come in?" he asks, and when she looks up it's clear they're not talking about the job.

"I told you I would."

"For a while there I wasn't sure."

"I always do what I say I'm going to. You should know that by now."

"I should," he says, reminded once again that he's the one who couldn't stop himself from constructing their perfect, imaginary future together, the one who made ridiculous promises and vows, the one who asked her to marry him. She'd laughed, then a week later cried after they made love, only to slam the bathroom door in his face. It still makes no sense to him: With her temper, she's the stable one. Maybe, as he sometimes thinks, he was crazy, and entirely mistaken about her, and should be grateful he's with Deena. Maybe he's still crazy.

Roz comes over with a drink tray tucked under one arm. "Look what Coach gave me." She dangles a twenty in front of Jacquie's nose, then snatches it away, folds it into her breast pocket and pats it.

"What did you do?" Jacquie needles.

"Is he still here?" Manny asks, swiveling, and spots him crossing the dining room.

He catches him at the coatrack and walks him out beside the live tank in his puffy jacket and Greek fisherman's cap, shaking his hand a last time before Coach tugs on his gloves.

"We'll beat Southington," Manny says.

"You know something I don't?"

"We always do."

"There's always a first time." Coach looks around the foyer, hands open as if to point out the decor. "It's going to be strange. The Olive Garden, huh?"

"Yeah. Come on by. We'll take care of you."

"I know you will. Take care of yourself, huh?"

"You too," Manny says, and because the lights are blinking, they wish each other a Merry Christmas. "Hard-hittin'—"

"New Britain."

Outside, in the snow, Mr. K. looks back and waves a last time. Manny waves and then watches him shuffle to his car the way he would his own abuelito, hoping all the while that he put down enough ice melter.

"It's official," Dom announces, hitching a thumb at the TV, "it's a blizzard. Winter Storm Adrian. New York's completely shut down."

"Damn," Manny says, as if impressed, but underneath he's wondering what impact that might have on tonight. He's been counting on this one last shift for so long, as if it might hold some final answer. It can't, he knows, yet he feels threatened by the idea of losing his last chance.

"Since when do winter storms have names?" Roz asks, then touches Manny on the elbow and leans into him. "We've got a problem on 16."

One of the office party's tables. A man bit into a cheddar biscuit and felt something thin and smooth like plastic wrap. The way Roz describes it, en route, Manny fears that Eddie lost one of his Band-Aids, lawsuit territory if there ever was.

The man has saved the evidence for Manny, handing him the bread-and-butter plate as if only he can identify the foreign object. The whole table looks to him. The plastic is flimsy and transparent—unlike, say, the fingertip of a glove—and pliable, not like cellophane.

"It's plastic wrap, all right," Manny says, flattering the guy's powers of deduction. "Sometimes we wrap the batter to keep it fresh. I'm very sorry. We'll be more than happy to take care of your meal." It takes Roz a second to find him in the POS. Manny makes a show of initialing the printout and giving it back, a leader signing an important treaty. The guy seems placated, shrugging as if it was an honest mistake. "If there's anything you want or need, please just ask and we'll do our best. Can I get you another Corona?"

"Sure."

"Lime with that?"

"Yes."

And Manny's off, handling the situation personally,

taking the offending plate with him—straight out of the old intern manual he used to study like a Bible when he was just breaking in: Remove food item in question—which he shows to Rich and Eddie, since they've both been baker today. "Who knows," he says, "it could have been me. I mixed the batter in the first place. We've all got to watch what we're doing."

"Yes, Chef," Ty tries, but Manny doesn't think it's funny.

He delivers the beer, almost salaaming, and the man thanks him—a sign that everything's cool. Bow-tie boss is fine, back to chatting with the guest of honor, and Manny decides to bounce instead of pushing it with a double table touch.

Up front, Kendra's standing with her face inches from the front doors, watching something outside. "Someone's stuck," she says, and he lifts a hand to black out the reflection and sees Mr. K.'s dinosaur of an Olds sideways across the lanes and struggling in the slush.

"Motherfuckers," Manny allows himself once he's outside—meaning the plow guys, still missing in action. The Olds revs and its tires whine. Rear-wheel drive is useless in this shit, and the old boat must weigh a couple of tons. Coach is just digging a hole, sending up an ozone of smoked rubber.

Manny slaps at the passenger window and shows him the bag of ice melter. "Let me put some of this down and I'll give you a push."

He stalls for a few seconds to give the pellets a chance to work. "Okay, now put it in reverse and just let it roll back a foot." He throws some in front of the wheels on both sides, then coaxes him forward with a hand, stops him. "Okay, now back again. Okay. Now straighten out the wheel. All right, let's give it a try."

Manny heaves against the trunk of the Olds as Coach inches it forward. His work shoes are treadless and don't grab, so he digs the sides of his heels into the snow like starting blocks. By now all the wheelspinning has built up an icy hump they have to clear. Between the ice melter, Manny getting some leverage and Coach nursing the gas pedal, they nearly have enough momentum, but at the last second they start to fall back, and Coach can't help but gun it, shooting twin streams of slush past Manny, swinging the back end to one side. The next try's the same. "Wait," Manny says, holding up a hand, but Coach doesn't hear him, and goes again. He's just making it worse.

"Try and rock it," Manny says, because one of the holes is a good foot long now and the melter seems to be working.

Coach rolls it back, then chunks it into drive, rolls it back, almost clearing the rear of the hump, then rocks forward, the tires catching asphalt and traction as Manny shoulders the trunk, the taillights flaring red in his face, and finally pushes weakly off the bumper as the Olds climbs and surges free, leaving him nothing but air to hang on to, and he falls on his hands and knees in the slush. He pushes up, swearing, cuffs and pants soaked. Mr. K.'s afraid of getting stuck again and doesn't slow, just honks, turns at the end of the row and rolls through the stop sign onto the plowed access road and away.

"Aw, man," Manny says, arms out to check the damage. His tie is ruined, he's wet and freezing, but he also feels like he's won something, being able to pay Coach back in some small way. The snow is falling softly— Charlie Brown snow—and there's almost no wind. It may just be the lull before the heavy stuff, but, waggling his hands at his sides to warm them, he thinks it's too pretty to be a blizzard.

Inside, he cleans up in the men's room, rinsing his tie, lifting his knees like a drum major so the blower can dry his pants. He polices the sinks with toilet paper, finger-rolling a wad into the trash before washing his hands. Less than a minute later, he scoops a wayward french fry off the floor by the kid's table and has to wash them again, and then again after he wipes down a drink-and-dessert menu the big party somehow gobbed with tartar sauce.

Lunch is under control, for now. The big party's finally quiet, busy eating their entrees. The kid is sitting still, gobbling down popcorn shrimp. It's one fifteen and the snow is keeping people away. Here it is the last day and he's still sweating the guest count; with the holiday crowd he was hoping for a packed house, just to shove it in corporate's face. Kendra seats the stragglers, then, with nothing to do, gives in and clears Roz's last four-top. The kitchen's caught up; Ty's already put Eddie and Leron back on dishes. Fredo's clearing the line, Rich is cleaning the baker's table. Sensing a chance to get ahead, Manny tries the plow guys, gets the machine again and leaves a second message, checks to see if his tie is drying—it's not—then glumly putters around the bar, watching with Dom as the white and pink storm sweeps across both screens.

Jacquie finds him eating beer nuts—something she tried to get him to cut down on—and he ditches the rest of the handful on a napkin as if he's done.

"We got any lighthouse glasses left?"

"How many you need?"

"It's got to be a special one, number seven or something, I don't know."

"We've only got the one."

He leads her to the stockroom, reaches up and takes down a cardboard box from the top shelf and undoes the wedged-together flaps. Side by side, they peer into it like a treasure chest. In a nest of tissue paper rest a dozen heavy molded glasses lumpy as ice sculptures—ugly, Manny's always thought, despite having seen them go for thirty dollars on eBay. The company offered a series of ten, but that was last year. The only people interested in them now are collectors; headquarters sent out a memo this spring warning against selling them outright. The rules still apply: The guest has to buy the right meal.

Just as Manny remembered, they're all number threes, an octagonal rocket that's supposed to be the Tybee Island Lighthouse in Georgia—so famous he's never heard of it. He leaves the box down so when Jacquie comes back he can wrap the glass again and fit it into its spot. Another thing to inventory.

The stockroom isn't a room at all but a hallway behind the grill with shelves on each side rising to the ceiling. As he waits, surrounded by identical drumlike cans of Sysco pickles and sliced mushrooms, plastic five-gallon jars of ketchup and honey mustard and cocktail sauce, Manny hears Ty riding Fredo ("That's not where that goes. Move out the way"), the transformerlike hum of the ice maker and the cyclic rinsing of the dishwasher. She kissed him here a dozen different times, mashed into him against his half-joking protests that they'd get caught. Some of the dustier cans probably witnessed them—the maraschino cherries and baby corn, maybe. It seems wrong that even these perishables have outlasted what he thought was eternal—still thinks, really—but there they are, solid evidence. The glasses too, even though they were supposed to be a limited offer. What isn't? He needs to remember that with Deena.

In a minute Jacquie's back without the glass. "She says she'll take all of them."

"They're one to a customer," he says, a reflex, and realizes from her look that he's being stupid. "Sure, whatever."

She gives him a different look when he takes one for himself.

"I can't believe you're really going to miss this place."

I can't believe you won't, he wants to say, but just shrugs. "I guess I've been here too long."

"I guess so."

He doesn't know why this is a joke (it's a lie, first off), but like all of his exchanges with Jacquie lately, he tries not to analyze it too closely, since it will come to nothing. They're just talking.

"What are you going to do?" he asks.

"Get a job—what do you think?"

"After today I'm not taking Crystal, so . . ."

"Manny," she stops him. "I thought we already talked about this."

"We did—"

"Don't start this again. Not now."

"I should have told you before—"

But here's Rich coming up behind her like a ghost. "Sorry. We need more oil."

"S'okay," Manny says, letting him squeeze past, but Jacquie's already walking away. He could run to catch her, even with the box in his arms. Instead, he walks them to the break room, carefully backing through the door, and unpacks them on the table for her.

"Thank you," she says.

"You're welcome."

"She'll be very happy."

"Yeah."

Roz stiff-arms in with a full bus tub, catching just the last of this. She shakes her head theatrically, as if he's making a big mistake, and keeps going, into the kitchen, hollering, "Got another present for you, Eddie."

Nicolette pushes through after her, holding a knife and a spoon and swearing under her breath. "Here. If someone's throwing their silverware on the ground, do you take it away from them or give them more?"

"Give them more," Manny says.

"For real. You do that in the nursing home, you don't get it back. And you definitely don't get dessert."

"He's eating dessert?"

"He's out there right now, going on his third spoon."

It's overkill, a second table touch on a four-top, but he can justify it as a follow-up on the spill. While the moms have their coffee and compare their lists, the kid's tackling a Fudge Overboard, a mountain of brownie, ice cream and aerosol whip smothered in chocolate sauce. Manny's seen guys his size quit on it, but the kid's half-way done and still shoveling.

"How was everything today?" Manny asks the moms.

"Good," the kid's mother says, "though I do think our server could have been more courteous." She looks to the other mother, who confirms it. "She seemed to have a problem with Martin, even before his accident. I think a restaurant that advertises itself as a family place should be prepared to deal with children."

"I understand," Manny says, but stops short of apologizing. Any other day he'd probably comp the kid's dessert, but for all her attitude, in this case Nicolette's right. He's not going to reward Mom for letting the kid run wild. "Would you mind filling out one of these comment cards? Thanks. Next time you're here we'll take special care of you, okay? You have a good day now."

"What an idiot," he tells Nicolette in the break room.

"And you know they're going to screw me. After all that bullshit."

"I got her to fill out a comment card."

"You didn't."

"I did. You can call her around four in the morning and read it back to her."

Nicolette jumps from her chair and pumps a fist. "Unh! Yeah, son! I know someone who's getting some late-night takeout. Get the door, it's Domino's, bitch!"

Manny puts a finger to his lips, and she chills. This is their secret, a breach of the rules that could get them both in trouble, but worth it. As big a pain in the ass as Nicolette is, she's still one of his servers.

When he swings back into the bar, Dom asks if he still wants the beer nuts.

"Toss 'em," Manny says, and has Dom run him a Diet Coke with lemon. Lunch is winding down, and he needs a shot of caffeine, especially with the day so dark. His cuffs are still damp, covering the rubber band. He takes the glass to the window and peeks between the blinds. Snow streaks past sideways as if he's riding a train, and he wonders how it looks from the back window of his apartment—the yard that slopes down to the creek a perfect white except for the dotted line of a cat's tracks. He imagines lying on the couch under his old Patriots sleeping bag all day tomorrow and watching the games, not even getting dressed, leaving his dishes around like he's sick. No, he needs to be here, he needs to see Deena. If he leaves her place right after dinner he might make it back to catch the end of the late game. And that quick it will be Monday and all of this will be history.

Outside, a skinny dude in a hoodie with his hands jammed in the pouch skirts the lower edge of the lot, hunched against the wind. He ignores the stop sign and crosses the road, headed for the mall. Where the hell did he come from? Not the front door—Manny would have seen him leave—and for an instant he thinks it's the homeless guy who gave them problems this fall, hunting for unlocked cars and climbing the fence to the dumpster. It's only when the figure stops to let an SUV back out and the brake lights show his face that Manny recognizes Fredo.

"What the fuck."

He clacks his glass down and hustles outside, the ball of keys banging at his hip. The ice melter's worked, but only to the end of the walk. Three steps into the lot, his shoes fill with slush and he has to retreat. "Fredo!" he calls into the blizzard. "Fredo!" With the snow it's hard to see, but he swears Fredo looks back once, just briefly, before going on, making straight for the bus shelter by JCPenney. "Okay," Manny hollers, arms stretched wide as if calling him out, "you can forget about your check."

The first thing Manny does is make sure he's punched out, which he is.

"I don't know," Ty says. "He just took off his apron and left."

"You didn't say anything to him?"

"Like what?"

Like: Are you really that stupid, or are you purposely trying to fuck this up? Like: Who told you to do that, because it sure as hell wasn't me. Like: Now I'm going to have to replate the whole thing, which is a waste of my fucking time.

"Did *anyone* try to stop him?"

Rich and Leron and Eddie look over but don't say a word, as if this doesn't concern them. Jacquie pushes in to refill a pitcher at the coffee station and watches them, sensing the drama.

"Fuck Frito," Ty says. "Eddie can handle backup."

"Aren't you the one that told me we couldn't do dinner with three people?" Manny asks.

"You really think we're going to serve dinner?"

"We're going to be open for whoever shows up."

"Then we'll be fine," Ty says, "because no one's gonna show up."

Manny can't dispute this, the way it's snowing, but he won't lose this argument either. When logic fails, a manager can always pull rank. "Someone's going to show up, and if no one does, we're still going to be ready for them. We're still in business, and we're still getting paid. I didn't come in today to play babysitter. Now let's get these desserts out and get this place squared away."

As halftime speeches go, this one doesn't inspire much of a response. Ty wanders back behind the hot plate, Rich tagging after him. Eddie and Leron turn away and silently unload the bus tubs and rack the dishes at their regular pace.

"You knew something like that was going to happen," Jacquie says in the break room.

"What?" Manny says, though he knows what she's going to say. He hired Fredo (as he hired Leron), seeing in him the ghost of his younger self—another lost New Britain kid at the bus stop, going nowhere. He gave Fredo a chance, and no matter what, he'll never consider that a mistake. He wants to believe that with another cook—someone with more patience and less of a temper—Fredo would have made it, but he's never worked with a cook like that. Honestly, a cook like that probably doesn't exist. The only person who would put up with Fredo's slowness is Manny himself.

"I'm surprised he came in," Jacquie says.

"I'm surprised anyone came in," Manny says. "I'm surprised I came in."

"Why do you have to go and make a joke about it? I don't know if you know this, but a lot of us only came in because of you."

"Like you."

"Yes like me. You think I came in because I got nothing better to do? Yeah, right, I'm here for the big money. Jesus, Manny, think for once."

She blasts him and walks away, something she has practice at, just as he has practice at turning her words over, trying to see what they really mean, and then holding that meaning at a distance, since everything between them is tentative and temporary, like the fine print on the menu says, subject to change without notice.

Roz swings in shouldering a tray of lipstick-smudged wine glasses and peeled beer bottles and gives him a sympathetic frown commonly reserved for toddlers, pouting with her bottom lip out. "Uh-oh. Looks like there's trouble in paradise."

"This is paradise?" Manny asks.

"Could be if you play your cards right."

She says it in passing, and is well into the kitchen when he lets out a single uncensored laugh, shaking his head at her ability to tease him as much as the ridiculous idea that he ever had cards to play.

Out front, the kid is leaving. Nicolette's boxed Mom's leftovers in a styrofoam clamshell and returned her credit card, said her good-byes and fled for the break room. Only now, with her Visa safe in her wallet, does the mother slide the comment card into the hinged leather folder, setting it beside the tea light. Manny lurks at the main wait station, watching them file past the grandmothers, who turn as one to remark on the boy, the only child in the whole place. Manny resists the urge to go over and placate the woman further—not hard, considering the kid is jumping around her legs like a hyper poodle.

Now they've stopped. One of the grandmothers wants to offer the kid something from her purse—a piece of hard candy, just what he needs.

"Keep moving," Manny murmurs to himself.

The mother's politely declining—no, thank you, we couldn't possibly—when the kid puts a hand to his mouth as if to cover a burp, bends at the waist and gushes all over her boots. A big butterscotch-colored flood, with chunks. And he's not done. The gagging is audible over Kenny Loggins, making one side of the retirement party turn in their chairs.

"Get him outside," Manny quietly urges, but the mother and her friend are trying to comfort the boy, not manhandle him to the door, and with their help he empties himself onto the carpet while the grandmothers gawk at one another, scandalized.

"Can *someone* please get him a glass of water?" the mother shouts, stuck in the puddle, since borrowing one of the grandmothers' is out of the question.

Manny has a pitcher right there at the station, and a spare goblet.

"*Thank* you," the mother scolds him.

"We'll take care of this here," he counters. "You can clean up in the restroom." But first he needs to wipe off the uppers of her boots so she doesn't track goop through the whole place. He kneels and wets a napkin in the ice water. Close up, the stuff smells like a mix of sour milk and fresh dog shit.

"Be careful," the woman says. "Don't soak them."

Lady, he wants to say, they're *boots*.

While he scrubs the stinking rug and fills a bus tub with nasty rags, Nicolette has to relocate the grandmothers to a booth as far away as possible, which is the equivalent of seating and serving them again. Jacquie takes a tray over. So does Kendra, as Roz shares an open-mouthed look of surprise with him. While he's down there, he notices a couple spots of gum on the underside of the table, and before he can stop himself, he thinks he should find the putty knife later and take care of them.

He's just breaking out the disinfectant spray when the mother stops him. The kid and the other mother are waiting by the live tank, the colored lights playing over their faces.

"I want to know who your supervisor is."

"I don't have a supervisor, I'm the manager."

"Okay, let me make this easier for you." She speaks precisely, enunciating each word as if he might have trouble understanding. "Who do I have to write to to complain about what happened here? Because I don't think a child being sick is something to laugh at, and I saw at least one of your employees laughing at my son."

"I'm sure that's not the case."

"I'm sure that *is* the case, and I *am* going to write a letter to someone about this."

"I can give you another comment card."

"I don't want another comment card. I want the name and address of someone who's actually going to do something."

Manny's tempted—as he's never been before—to tell her her kid's a brat and that she's a terrible mother, and a terrible human being, but instead he gives her the contact info for the regional director and apologizes just to get her out the door. He smiles and eats a big shit sandwich in front of everyone, and if they don't understand, Manny does: Like his face-off with Ty, it's just the cost to be the boss.

The wetted carpet reeks like an overpowering cheese. He fogs the spot with disinfectant, then spends a couple minutes at the hygiene sink washing his hands. Once the mess dries he'll vacuum, but not with guests present. The idea is to let things settle, let them all forget. Impossible in real life, and yet here it works perfectly. In fact, once the kid and his mom are gone, an infectious laughter circles the room as if they've all been holding it in, the grandmothers included, hooting and slapping the table-top so hard their silverware rattles.

Manny needs to let it go too. The big party's done, and Jacquie and Roz can use a hand settling their checks. He fingers the screen of the POS, swiping cards and printing slips. In another idiocy of corporate procurement, the system is brand-new. He likes the speed and the neatness of the transactions, and the feeling of completion, of closing the deal, money in the till, as if it somehow counts in his favor. At the Olive Garden, as assistant manager, his receipts will blend in, just one ingredient in a larger pot, and, aware of how selfish it sounds, since he's always preaching teamwork, he thinks that's a loss.

As the party filters out, Manny posts up by the host stand, following protocol, and thanks them as they pass, a kind of receiving line, Kendra behind him like a bride, reminding them to drive safely. The boss in the bow tie shakes his hand. "Thanks for getting us in on such short notice."

"Not a problem. Thanks for thinking of Red Lobster."

By now he says this as a reflex, but what does it mean? Who, besides the people who actually work here, thinks about Red Lobster? And even they don't really think about it. Maybe Eddie, who seems happy to have a place to come every day, or Kendra, who doesn't always, but Manny can't imagine Rich or Leron wasting much thought on what's just a job. Maybe Manny didn't think enough of it either, all the years he took for granted that the Lobster would be here. In that way, he thinks, he's just like Eddie. And now it's too late.

Like they did on the way in, the party bunches up under the marlin, the snow outside an obstacle. One by one they retrieve their jackets from the coatrack (one woman, strangely, carries an umbrella) and button up before braving the storm, then leave in waves, leaning on one another for balance, and again Manny wonders what it would be like to work there—or anywhere else, really, since it's obvious he can't waste his whole life working for Darden Restaurants, Incorporated.

When the last of them are gone, he notices an ornament on the floor by the live tank, an ancient pink-and-cream-striped bulb cracked in pieces like a bird's egg, the largest showing its shiny silver insides. It's something that might have come from his abuelita's tree. Someone must have brushed against it and not heard it hit the carpet. The irony bothers Manny: something so delicate that had survived so many Christmases; one more day and it would have made it. Or maybe what bugs him is how sentimental he's getting, seeing his own fate in every little thing, as if he's helpless. He grabs the push sweeper from beside the host stand and rolls it back and forth until all the shards are gone, then deposits them in the kitchen garbage, knocking the head against the rim to empty it.

"Easy there, chief," Ty says. "You break it you bought it." He's perched on a stool at the end of the grill, leafing through the *Courant* while Rich works the ass end of the dishwasher in rubber gloves, pulling burning plates off the racks and stacking them in rollaways.

"You guys all done with lunch?"

Ty holds both arms wide to show off the spotless counter.

"What's our dinner special?"

"Whatever's left."

"Make it lobster tails," Manny says, hoping they can get rid of some. "What's for lunch?"

"Whatever you make," Ty says, but Manny's not going for the joke. "Whatever people want. I've got some snow-crab legs—if we're not saving them for dinner."

"I've got to go to the mall, but make sure everyone gets something." Meaning Roz, who'll drink coffee instead of eat. Even at 50 percent off, the food's not a bargain. Sometimes a manager's got to exercise his discretion. "And tell everyone it's free today."

"Nice," Rich says, giving him a gloved thumbs-up.

"Sure you want to leave me in charge?" Ty asks.

"Who else is there?"

"I'll be in charge," Eddie says. "I'll give everybody a raise."

"Okay, Guapo," Manny surrenders, "you're in charge."

Out front the grandmothers are taking their time, asking Nicolette for refills on coffee, oblivious of the fact that they're the only customers. Or maybe they're afraid to go outside; the snow's drifting against the concrete legs of the benches, the wind sending snakes skirling off across the lot. Dom is predicting two feet for this stretch of 84, more in the western hills.

"I think we're basically screwed," he says, "if we weren't already."

"If people can't drive," Manny reasons, "they've got to stop somewhere."

"Not if they never leave home in the first place."

Manny points to the windows. "It's not even three o'clock."

"So how long do you wait before you call dinner?"

"What, you got a date or something?" Manny says, then, arbitrarily, "Four thirty."

Kendra's restless, and Nicolette's frustrated with the grandmothers, now trying to pay their checks with expired two-fer coupons. With no one else in the place, Manny can hear her laying down the law from across the room. "I'm sorry, ma'am, even if this coupon *was* valid, that offer's only good for one meal per table, not two." Logically, Nicolette's got them, but the grandmothers keep pleading their case. The volume escalates, and Manny has to step in.

The grandmothers insist they're two tables, since they asked for separate checks, and the coupon's barely expired. Nicolette hands it to him as if it's dipped in anthrax. The expiration date is last Saturday, close enough, except as he's standing there he notices the ceramic holder that should be full of sugar and Equal and Splenda and Sweet'n Low packets has been picked clean—always a danger with these cottonheads, their memories of the Depression pushing them beyond thrift into greed. It shouldn't matter to him, since anything not in a sealed box will probably get tossed, but now he feels doubly fooled.

"One table, one entree," he rules, and short-circuits

their arguments with a raised finger. "And I'm only do-ing this because it's Christmas."

"I'm never eating here again," one of them says.

"I thought this was supposed to be a nice place."

"I'm sorry you feel that way," Manny says. "You can fill out a comment card if you like."

Back at the main station, Nicolette says he shouldn't have given them anything. "Bet you twenty they don't tip me."

"Too easy," Manny says, and then is wrong. The grandmothers leave Nicolette a single penny—a penny Nicolette runs to the front door and flings into the storm after them. "Fuckin' old biddies, I hope you crash!"

She still has to clear their coffees, but steams straight for the break room, empty-handed and swearing. As her tantrums go, this one's minor. It's only when she reap-pears a minute later in her jacket with her bag over her shoulder that he realizes she's serious.

"Let them go," he says.

"I want my check."

"No you don't."

"You want to see how much I made today?" She threatens him with a folded wad of ones. There can't be more than twenty dollars.

"It's been slow."

"It wasn't slow for everybody, was it? Just me. Now why would that be?" She scratches her temple, then holds a flattened palm out like a game-show model toward Kendra, standing at the bar with Dom, then bends it toward Manny. He deserves this, partly, for keeping her away from the big party, and he can't promise to make it up to her at dinner. "I shouldn't be surprised. I mean, one of them's your girlfriend and the other's your mother, so right there that leaves me out. I don't mind working a crappy shift as long as I have a fair shot at making some money, and you know that's true 'cause I worked every fucking lunch for the last month straight when I could have just said fuck you. I knew you were shorthanded. That's why I came in today, and look what I get. So that's it, I'm done. All I want is to get my check and get the fuck out of here. You don't need me anyway."

"I gave you good shifts too," Manny says.

Nicolette just stands there, adamant, admitting nothing. He knows he's supposed to ask her to stay, maybe beg her, but lunch is over, there's no one here and the snow is falling hard.

"I'll get you your check," he says. "You already punch out?"

"Yes."

And in back she has; it wasn't a bluff.

Jacquie and Roz already know, sitting at the table in the break room as if nothing's wrong.

"Oh well," Jacquie says.

"It's not like she did anything around here anyway,"

Roz says, and he thinks maybe he's soft-hearted, because he wants them to miss her.

He wants to shake Nicolette's hand, as if to settle things between them, but she just takes the check, slips it in her bag and pulls on her gloves. Like Fredo, she has to make the trek to the bus stop, and she's already bundled up. Kendra and Dom haven't budged, so they have an audience as Manny escorts her to the door.

"Thanks," he says in the semiprivacy of the vestibule, and not just from habit. She did work for him, and he does appreciate it.

"Fuck you," Nicolette says. "You fired me instead of Crystal—that's what it comes down to—and do you see Crystal anywhere? No, but here I am like an idiot, so just fuck you, Manny. *Thanks,*" she mocks him, her final word.

As always, he's aware of a crowd at his back. He knows they can't hear everything, but he also knows the glassed-in box will broadcast the tone of his reply like a drum. He wants to say he didn't fire anyone, that he fought hard for those five spots, and that, honestly, he would have taken anyone ahead of her, even Le Ly, who could barely speak English.

"Good luck," he says as she pushes into the storm, and gives her a stiff salute of a wave. Watching her go, he thinks it's wrong that instead of sadness or anger, all he feels is a selfish, indifferent relief. It feels—in this case, at least—like he's admitting defeat.

When he comes back in, Kendra asks if she can have her check, and instead of telling her she can leave too, without a word he goes to the safe and gets all the checks except his and hands them out, throws his coat on and stalks right by Roz and Jacquie—Roz calling, "Hey, don't go away mad!"—and through the deserted dining room and past the vacant host stand, bulling through the vestibule and into the whipping, whirling snow, striding away without looking back, sliding in his useless shoes (yes, he's going to have to deal with the snowblower), thin socks already wet, following Nicolette's half-filled tracks across the lot toward the dark, spotlit block of the mall. Without thinking, he strips the rubber band off his wrist and fires it into the air, where it disappears among the flakes. This is what quitting must feel like, Manny thinks, this righteous exhilaration, but by then it's evaporating and he's tired, across the access road and slogging along in the cold. He still needs to deal with Deena's present, a question he's put off too long already. Helplessly he remembers pinching the tiny silver clasp of the necklace open to put it on Jacquie that first time, Jacquie bending her head forward, gathering up her hair with one hand so he could see the wispy beginnings of it, and the knob at the top of her spine, the freckle next to it a perfect circle.

A blade bangs down and a big diesel roars, the scraping so close he could swear it's going to run him over, but no, it's just a trick of the snow and the weird, muffled quiet. There's nothing behind him but empty spaces, a few parked cars drifted to the hubcaps. The truck's all the way across the road, peeping then lunging forward again, its headlights sweeping across the Lobster like it's opening night. The plow guy has arrived.

THE MOST WONDERFUL TIME

The mall swallows him. He swings through the first bank of chromed doors, wipes his shoes on the ribbed rubber matting and swings through the second set into a tepid, empty hallway. Like the Lobster, the Willow Brook Mall isn't new, and the overhead fluorescents are as dim as the kitchen's, and dully reflected underfoot. Somewhere a brass ensemble pipes a dirgelike "Good King Wenceslas," otherwise the only signs of life are two WET FLOOR pyramids like tiger's teeth—CUIDADO: PISO MO-JADO, translated too late for his abuelita, with a feature-less stick figure falling back, one leg straight out, the other bent at the knee, a hand thrown up Travolta-like, as if he's dropping into a break-dance or sliding home. A connoisseur of mopping, Manny notices it's a slapdash job, wet-mopped but not rinsed so the dirt is drying in a switchbacked ribbon, yet out of professional respect he detours around it.

The first sixty feet of hallway is all wall. The first stores on both sides are closed, though not because of the snow—

they're vacant: dark, carpeted boxes fenced with barred grilles, a larger, more polite form of the corrugated garage doors used to protect storefronts in the city. The space on the right was a tux place called Finest Formals, the one on the left a travel agency, he thinks, maybe a Shawmut Bank before that. Whatever it was, it didn't last long.

Far ahead, toward the heart of the mall, backlit by the bright atrium in front of Penney's, a few shoppers glide like shades, one a mother with a stroller. So people are still open, a good sign. He zeroes in on the three-sided kiosk of a directory, striding fast—he only has half an hour for his lunch break—then stopping dead to search the floorplan of the mall, sectioned and color-coded like a child's game board.

His mission is simple: Buy something she will love, and love him for buying. Nothing useful, like a new camera to take pictures of the baby (that's on a different list), or a brake job for her Elantra (on no list but his, nagging as a jagged cavity or the sudden absence, now, of the rubber band). It has to be intimate yet unexpected, arrived at by magic, a consumer version of mind reading. Price isn't an issue, within limits. Manny's thinking a hundred, a hundred-fifty, leaning toward the extravagant on principle. He needs this to be good.

So, clothes? Right now she doesn't have a size, and even when he's buying for himself he doesn't trust his taste.

Perfume? They all smell too strong to him, and the

top of her dresser is solid bottles. The odds of getting something she doesn't have and likes are slim.

Music? Too high school, not personal enough, the same with electronics.

Which leaves the fool's last resort: jewelry.

Mansour Jewelers is D11, tucked into the wing right beside Penney's, but that's where he bought Jacquie's necklace. He'll have to go all the way down the second level past Kmart and try Zales. Earrings, pearls or diamonds, as big as he can afford—a simple plan, yet he can't keep it in his head. On the escalator, angling above the cotton-wadded North Pole and its empty red-and-gold throne (a bad sign), a blankness comes over him, wiping his mind clean, a purposeful short circuit, like when he thinks of Jacquie laughing from her bathroom, or the branching crack in her ceiling, or how she looks when she's asleep. He willfully releases the memory, and creeping into the vacuum is a feeling of surrender, as if it's no use.

Everything's open on the second floor, but traffic is unnaturally sparse. He passes a pregnant woman by Hickory Farms, and then a minute later spies another below, eating a giant cookie beside a fountain glittering with pennies. On the far side of Kmart there are two more, and more strollers, more toddlers. It shouldn't surprise him—this is just who comes here, like the grandmothers lunching at the Lobster—but it forces him to question what he would have done if Jacquie had wanted the baby.

He said he wanted to marry her, and she laughed. He knows—he knew then—that that wasn't realistic, and yet he was ready to follow through with the rest of his life, honestly pledging himself, maybe because she never took him seriously. He hasn't asked Deena, and the way he feels now he doubts he ever will, and there's something wrong with that. He can just hear what his abuelita would say.

It's also the first Christmas he doesn't have to buy a gift for his lita—other than a wreath for the visit he keeps putting off—another absence that has him distracted. He has the needling, bad-dream feeling that he's supposed to get something else while he's here, but can't quite figure out what, or for whom. He wonders if Coach will be alone over Christmas, if maybe he should arrange to look in on him before he heads down to Deena's. Yes, definitely, he can set it up Monday at the Olive Garden, and while Manny has no idea what to get him either, just having a plan to concentrate on—something to work toward and look forward to beyond tonight—helps.

Or helps some. A manager, he's never free of his responsibilities. It may be his lunch break, a quiet halftime in the day, but even as he scans the display windows for something Coach might like, he's aware that every step takes him farther away from Jacquie and the Lobster—

away from the real world where his life waits—and that he's wasting what little time he has left there.

He's walked at least half a mile and is beginning to sweat lightly, but keeps his jacket on to hide his waistline. As he passes The Limited, lost in untangling these knots, a little girl in the doorway behind him laughs. She points at him, covering her mouth, and her mother has to grab her arm and lower it, flashing him an apologetic grimace, as if this happens all the time. He goes on, paranoid, sure that people are staring at him. It's possible his hair is wet from the snow and curling like a bad perm, and he pretends to look in the window of Old Navy and slicks it back with both hands, just in time to catch a pair of shaggy string-bean teens behind him turning their heads toward him in unison like in a scary movie, and then, when Manny wheels around, walking on as if he's invisible.

What the hell?

Since he's already there at the window, he twists to see if there's a KICK ME sign taped to his back and discovers that his jacket is ripped. No, not ripped, slashed, because when he pulls it off and holds it up to inspect the damage he can see someone's taken an incredibly sharp knife to the leather and split it cleanly all the way from the collar down to the belt in one long slice.

Fredo. Probably thought it was Ty's.

"Motherfucker," Manny says. And there's no way to fix it, it's done.

Fucking Fredo, can't even do this right. Now he can really forget about his check. Legally, Manny's not sure how that'll work, but right now he doesn't care. And right now there's nothing he can do about it, so he folds the jacket over his arm and keeps going. More than ever, he just wants to get this over with.

The Kmart isn't busy, but it never is. It's the second atrium that surprises him, the open space below set up for a choir—a makeshift stage with risers and music stands—but deserted, as if he's early for the show. The place looks evacuated. Only a female security guard sits in the audience of folding chairs, in the very last row, on the aisle, eating something from a piece of foil. Up here on the second level he's one of two shoppers, the other a white girl far across the opening, headed the other way as if fleeing him. When he enters the wing where Zales is, he has the hallway all to himself.

He expects it will be closed—his punishment for abandoning his post—and that he'll have to walk back past Mansour's and try again tomorrow, but a small blonde is standing behind the counter in a little black dress and lipstick, hair tucked behind her ears to show off a pair of simple diamond studs—exactly what Manny's come here for.

Even though they're the only two in the place, she lets him look around the glass counters for a minute before coming over.

"Ken I halp you vit samtink?"

Like anyone who grew up in New Britain, Manny can recognize a Polish accent. JADWEGA, her nametag says. She sounds new to America, but she's beautiful—blue-eyed and delicately built—and supremely confident. "For a gehlfriend, is?"

She doesn't need many words to steer Manny to a pair of diamonds like her own for $179 ("Dese mek her very heppy"), and before Manny realizes he's been flirting with her, he asks her to model them. She does, turning in profile, holding a manicured hand with blood-red nails to her neck like on QVC, one way and then the other. On Deena they'll look completely different, but that doesn't matter. They'd look different on Jacquie too. Sometimes it's not the thought that counts, just the present.

"I'll take them," Manny says, and waits as she gift wraps the fancy box.

"Tenk you," she says, smiling, and sends him off, still slightly confused at what just happened, like someone waking from a spell. He can't imagine having that kind of power—the kind Jacquie had over him, still has—and thinks he'll always be helpless and stupid that way, uncool. But he has Deena's present, has it wrapped and bagged, the telltale receipt hidden in his wallet, and that's exactly what he came here to do, no matter how he got it done.

And done quickly—he still has another twelve minutes. Walking back, he sees a biker-looking dude on

crutches outside the Gingerbread House and remembers
Eddie wanted some lottery tickets. There's no place up-
stairs that would sell them, so he takes the escalator down
and cruises the main hallway. All he needs is a news-
stand, but there's only a useless Walden Books. Smoker's
World is closed. He can't believe no one in this entire mall
sells something as basic as lottery tickets, but the directory confirms it. The closest place is going to be one of
the gas marts by the highway—the Mobil beside Friday's,
or the Citgo next to Daddy's Junky Music, probably closer.
If he backtracks and cuts through Kohl's and goes out
the side by Ruby Tuesday's, he'll only have to walk part-
way across the lot.

And like that he decides to do it, a knight errant ac-
cepting a quest. He turns on his heel and heads back past
Weathervane and RadioShack and the empty stage. With
no strolling crowd to navigate, he's making great time.
He turns in to Kohl's and follows the maze of linoleum
aisles to the rear of the store, where the doors give on the
lot. It's almost dark, though his watch says it's just short
of four. A car passes with its lights on and its wipers
flipping, its wheels packed with snow. He pauses on the
wet matting between the doors to zip his ruined jacket,
wishing he had a hat, then mashes the crashbar and
bounces out.

Whoever salted did a shitty job. There's no line between the sidewalk and the lot, just a drop-off, the lip

interrupted by the smooth dip of a handicapped ramp. The snow is easily a foot deep, and Manny churns for the middle of the road, his socks already logged. Maybe this wasn't such a good idea. It's early—he can still turn back—but once he's in the lane it's okay. The Citgo's sign is lit, snow blowing through its halo. Trudging, waiting for a plow to come rumbling up behind him, he keeps it in sight like a mirage, afraid it will disappear. Flakes stream out of the darkness, making him blink, melting into his skin, and there's something elemental and pleasing about the feeling. Humping up the ramp, shoes slipping, fingers freezing, he's as happy as he's been all day.

The one car on the highway is a news van from Channel 30 with a satellite dish on top, its chains rattling. The road is furrowed and white. The lights clunk and change for no one.

The uniformed cashier at the Citgo is alone on her cell phone and doesn't seem surprised to see him shamble in out of the storm. Behind her on the wall are a dozen locked roll dispensers of flashy scratch-off tickets. He's never played the lottery—his lita always said it was for idiots like his Uncle Rudy—and has to ask the woman for a Powerball form. She doesn't stop talking, just points to a display with the current pot written in Magic Marker: $285 million.

9 Ways To Win, the form promises, and lists the odds. He has to choose five numbers between 1 and 55, then

one number between 1 and 42—the red Powerball number. Match them all and Eddie wins the grand prize.
Match the five white numbers and he wins a hundred
thousand dollars. Four white and the Powerball, five
thousand. The other six ways pay a hundred bucks or
less, not much of a thrill. Eddie said he had five, so
Manny will buy him five more, doubling his odds, but
what numbers should he pick? He knows the cashier can
just have the machine choose them at random, but that's
like not even playing.

For the first ticket, he picks 03 and 05 for March 5th,
the first time he kissed Jacquie, 08 and 11 for her birth-
day, 27 for her age, and for the Powerball 34, for David
Ortiz, the real Big Papi, her favorite player on the Red
Sox. The next one is Deena's, then one for his lita, one for
Eddie, one for Coach, each with its own secret code,
births and anniversaries, addresses and heroes—numbers that are already lucky, being loved.

The clerk puts her phone down to take his slip and
punch them in. The first ticket juts from a slot on the
top of the machine like at the movies, and Manny thinks
this is what must hook compulsive gamblers, because for
an instant the dream seems real—the possibility that
this freshly printed chit might hold a completely different future for all of them. The clerk hands him the
ticket and he thinks she's made a mistake. He wanted
five. He's about to say something when he realizes all of

his numbers are on it, squished in the center in blocky dot matrix, looking about as official as a coupon printed off the internet. While the clerk resumes her conversation, he stands there double-checking the numbers, then fits the awkward stub into his wallet with Deena's receipt, as if they're of equal value.

The walk back seems longer, and colder, or maybe he's just slower, ducking into the warm Kohl's and shedding his jacket, then pulling it on again by Penney's for the last bitter stretch to the Lobster, an outpost glowing in the distance. He's right on time—even now trying to lead by example, when there's no point. It's ten after four, a dead spot before the dinner service, so he's confused to see a van roll up to their stop sign, signal and then pull onto the access road, headed for the exit. In the gathering dusk and falling snow it's hard to make out, but as it turns, the white brow of the aerodynamic fairing on top of the cab, big outrigger mirrors and long, boxy cabin of a short bus are unmistakable. The windows will be tall and tinted, and while he can't see them this far away, he knows the stripes along the side are green and blue, twined with a snaking cartoon blacktop split by a dotted yellow line, and splashed over the rear quarter panel will be some funky *I Love the 70s* script urging him—too late, he thinks—to TAKE A RIDE ON EASY STREET.

PLEASE WAIT TO BE SEATED

A foot in the door, Kendra stabs him with the bad news. She has her jacket on, as if she was about to go out and search for him. Eddie's gone, and she's leaving. Her mother called from Bristol, saying they've lost power, and she needs to get home.

She doesn't owe him any loyalty, he supposes (now that she has her check), and he can greet, so it's okay. While part of him feels deserted, he wouldn't want his abuelita or Deena sitting alone in the dark either, if that's actually true.

"What happened with Eddie?" he asks, peeling off his jacket so she won't see the damage.

"I guess they were worried about the snow. It's supposed to get worse."

"Did somebody call?"

"They just showed up and said he had to go."

"We lose anybody else?"

"No, but I don't think you'll be serving dinner anyway."

"You never know," Manny says, smiling and shrugging as if it's a joke.

83

"I've gotta go," Kendra says, and this time he has a chance to shake her hand and thank her for all her work.

"Okay," she says, and backs away as if he's crazy. "I hope you guys get home safe."

"You too."

He doesn't watch her go, but cuts through the break room, the box from Zales in his pocket, hidden from Roz, who's doing the crossword and picking at a piece of Key lime pie.

"Whadja get?" she asks without looking up.

"It's a surprise," he says, and he's through the swinging door into the kitchen.

He goes to the coatrack to check on Ty's jacket. If his suspicions are correct, it'll be fine. Then he'll have to decide if it's worth telling anyone. He thinks it should be enough, holding Fredo's check and then not giving him a reference.

He grips the shoulder of Ty's coat and angles the hanger out. He can see a slice of powder blue through the back, slashed the exact same way.

Son of a bitch. After all he did for him.

Jacquie's is fine, and Roz's, Leron's army surplus. It's just his and Ty's, and while the evidence is obvious, Manny still wants to believe his was a mistake.

He finds Ty smoking by the open back door with Jacquie, his top two buttons undone. Snow floats in and melts on the tile floor. Officially they're supposed to be outside, but today it's close enough.

"How was the mall?" Jacquie asks.

"Still open."

"Lot of people there?"

"Some. It's really not that bad out."

He lights up and leans against the counter with them, tapping his ashes in the big sink, the wind reaching through the door, chilling him. "You guys eat?" he asks, but all he's doing is stalling. He wants to keep the jackets a secret from Jacquie (not just his, but both), as if they're an admission of failure.

"So Kendra's gone," he says. "Where's Rich and Leron?"

"Watching UConn," Ty says, and tips his head toward the bar.

"Women or men?"

"What's the difference?" Jacquie says, because she doesn't care.

"Men, against Syracuse."

They don't talk about tomorrow, or the Olive Garden, tacitly agreeing that these topics are too heavy for a lazy cigarette break. Basketball is easier, and busting on Kendra for bugging out early, and then remembering Suzanne, who was just crazy and evil. They laugh with the pride of survivors, the hardcore, and Manny's glad.

Finally Jacquie flicks her filter out the door and walks

the length of the kitchen to the break room. Manny watches her go, her tight dark hair shining under the lights. It's still a mystery, how she moves under her uniform—maybe even more of one now, or maybe it's just his own confusion, having been so close. The break room door swings closed and she's gone.

"I've got to show you something," he tells Ty.

First he shows him his own jacket. Ty tilts his out and shakes his head as if he should have known—"Fuckin' little bitch"—then shoves it in again and bounces out of the narrow hallway, heading straight for the back door, fast, as if he's going after Fredo. Manny follows, drawn on by his sheer speed.

Outside it's nighttime, the pale light above the dumpster glaring down, throwing shadows across the snow. The plow guy has done a half-assed job back here, clearing only the front row and a single exit lane around the corner. Manny's Regal and Ty's Supra are nearly drifted in. Several fading sets of footprints cross the untouched expanse: all of them to the dumpster but one, and these Ty follows, keeping to the side as if saving them for evidence. They dead-end between the two cars.

"You better be fucking kidding me," Ty says, angling for the gap.

Manny's thinking Fredo's keyed them. From behind, with the shadows, it's impossible to tell. The snow is still perfectly caked, describing the Regal's boxy trunk and the Supra's sloped fastback. The roofs are intact, and the hoods. Ty suddenly stops in front of him, fixed on something, and Manny has to peek over his shoulder.

In each crusted windshield gapes a dark hole the size of a fist. From Manny's sticks a handle with a turned wooden grip he half recognizes.

"What the fuck is this?" Ty says, and pulls out the macelike, silver head of the potato masher.

"He was on potatoes."

Ty holds the masher straight up like a hammer. "He is fucking dead."

The hole is ragged, the glass bashed and wrinkled all round it, as if Fredo had to beat on it till he broke through. Manny doesn't understand why anyone would hate him, yet he has the feeling that, partially at least, he's to blame for this. The dash is drifted with snow and sharp blue cubes. Ty's is the same, but on the passenger side, easier to drive. Manny doesn't say he's lucky.

"We should call the cops."

"Why?" Ty says. "They're not going to do anything."

"For insurance."

"It doesn't matter—it's glass. We should just go kick Fredo's ass. You've got a number for him, right?"

"We should cover these with something."

"You got a number for him?"

"I'm not sure if it's still good."

"Gimme it and we'll find out. Fuckin' Frito, man. I don't know why you ever hired him."

After what's happened, Manny can't defend him. "I don't either."

Once the initial shock wears off, they unlock their doors and clean up the glass and snow. Manny has experience at this. When his grandmother was alive, her car was stolen three times, right out of their driveway—just kids, joyriding—and he became an expert at making windows out of garbage bags and cardboard. A windshield's different, but he's got to get home sometime tonight. He knows there's a roll of duct tape and a box cutter in a plastic breadbasket in the storage closet, and like that he's off for the back door, grateful to be absorbed in solving the problem.

Dom catches him in the kitchen and tags after him into the stockroom. It's past four thirty. "So what's the story with dinner?"

"We're serving it."

Dom stops and lets him walk on.

Manny can feel him lurking and turns. Dom stands there, framed by the shelves, staring at Manny like he's insane. "You don't have to stay if you don't want to. I think it's going to be pretty slow tonight."

"I think you're right."

"It's your call. Whenever you want to leave, just let me know."

"I think I want to leave now, if that's okay."

"That's fine," Manny says, and advances on him. "Thanks for coming in. I know you didn't have to."

"No problem," Dom says. "If it wasn't for the weather . . ."

"I understand," Manny says, and grips his hand. "Have Roz and Jacquie tip you out."

"They already did."

"All right," Manny says, "take it easy," and while this good-bye feels cleaner than Kendra's, as he opens the closet and searches the mothball-smelling shelves for the breadbasket, he wonders why Dom bothered to ask. If Manny said he had to stay, would he have just said fuck you and quit? And why does that matter to him?

The duct tape is right where it should be but the box cutter's missing, and he has to detour around the break room and sneak behind Rich and Leron watching the game to steal Kendra's scissors from the host stand. One garbage bag is all he needs. He has it in hand, crossing the open floor of the kitchen, when Roz emerges from the walk-in. He sees her too late, swerving away from the threat out of reflex.

"Whatcha doin'?" she asks, poking a fork at all the gear. She has a second wedge of pie—her idea of lunch.

He keeps walking, hoping to get away. "Window broke."

"Where?" she asks, puzzled, because there are none in the kitchen.

"My car."

"What, did a tree fall on it?"

By now he's at the end of the line, turning for the back door. He waves. "It's all right, I got it."

He's halfway across the lot when he hears her call from the loading dock: "What happened?"

"See what fuckin' Frito did?" Ty hollers, arms wide.

After that, everyone has to see. They gather around like a crowd at an accident, Roz and Jacquie in their coats while Rich and Leron tough it out in shirtsleeves, swearing and smirking—half in sympathy, Manny thinks, and half in admiration of Fredo's balls. Manny doesn't have enough hands, and there's nowhere dry to set anything, so Roz and Jacquie take charge of the duct tape. Rich levels a flashlight at the glass while Leron hands Ty a square cut from a Dewar's carton. As Manny fits the bandage over the hole in the Supra's windshield, he realizes there's no one watching the Lobster, and panics for an instant, imagining a thief digging in the cash drawer, or, more likely, an older couple waiting by the host stand. And then, looking around at everyone pitching in, he thinks that's okay. This is better, all of them here together.

It gives him some momentum to work with when they

file back in, stamping their feet and hanging their coats in the back hall, taking a minute to gape at the matching leather jackets. They gather in a loose circle by the coffee station. Break's been over for twenty minutes, so they have to know what's coming.

"Okay," he says, gauging their faces. With the radio and the dishwasher off, he feels like he's onstage. "We're going to set up for dinner like usual, we're just going to go light. Roz and Jacquie, let's sit orange and pink. We can add on yellow if we have to." They nod as if this makes sense. "Ty, Rich, Leron, pretend we're prepping for a regular weekday lunch. We should already be solid on sides, right?"

"Yes, chef," Ty says.

"Come on, man," Manny says, almost whining, because he needs him to be serious.

"We're good."

"Okay," Manny says, with a little more volume, and claps once, sending them off—all but Ty, who stands there like Manny's forgotten something.

"Still waiting on those digits."

"You can try it," Manny shrugs, and pulls it up on his cell. Ty reads the screen and punches the number in, then retreats to the loading dock, the only place they get reception. Manny sees he has one voice mail, from Deena, an hour ago. He ducks into the stockroom to listen to it, partly so he won't hear Ty.

"Hey," Deena says, and pauses. "Just wanted to see what's up. I guess you're working. It's snowing really bad here. They're telling people not to drive." He's leaning against a shelf, head bent, when he registers a change of light to his left, a dark shape in the doorway—Jacquie sneaking in for some sugar packets. He waves with his free hand, but she's already turned away. "—bad accident on 95, but it should be okay by tomorrow. Gimme a call and let me know what time you're going to be here. I want to get a tree. And be careful going home. Okay, later."

When he comes out, Ty's banging a saucepan down on the stovetop.

"Any luck?"

"Fuck no. You got an address for him?"

"No," Manny says.

"Call the cops then, I don't care."

So Manny does, sticking his head out the back door, giving their information. The dispatcher sounds unimpressed, as if he's wasting her time.

"With the weather situation there's nothing we can do about it right now. Will somebody be there tomorrow?"

"I'll be here," Manny says, then pockets the phone.

A kitchen is about pacing, everyone meshing at the same speed. The hardest thing is starting from zero. As always, Manny tries to lead by example. He gets the radio going and stands shoulder to shoulder with Leron, skew-

ering garlic shrimp, when really he should be snowblow-
ing the front walk. Any other day, he'd savor this lull, the
kitchen a warm cocoon against the bad weather, and he
thinks it's a shame to let everything else ruin it.

The marinade is slippery, and a shrimp squirts out of
Manny's gloved hand and lands on the clean brushed
steel, leaving a spicy smear. He pitches it in the garbage
and wipes the table with a rag. Leron just keeps working,
nimbly picking and poking, piling his finished spears in
their shared chafing dish. Manny gets back into rhythm
again, trying to match him, and does for a while, pressing, eventually falling behind. Leron shows no sign of
noticing, though he must. Manny glances over at the
mouse under his eye, the top of his cheek pinched and
swollen, and for the tenth time today wonders what he's
doing here. He's tempted to give him Warren's spot at the
Olive Garden, except there's no way he'd make it there,
coming in late or stoned or both (and Manny's not being
a hypocrite: There's a right time and a wrong time to be
stoned). In fact, he looks stoned now, eyes red-rimmed, a
capillary meandering out of one corner like an oxbowed
creek. Probably got high while Manny was at the mall,
probably not alone either. Still, he feels the urge to reward him—Rich too—but how?

Standing there thinking, he's fallen even further behind, and it's past five, officially dinner. He watches Leron, shaking his head at his speed.

"Too fast for me," he says, pinching off his gloves. "I'm going to go fight that snowblower."

"All right," Leron says.

"Need help?" Ty needles from the grill, because he knows the battles they've had.

" 'F I do I'll let you know."

"I'll send out a search party."

"Better send CSI, 'cause I'll kill the thing if it doesn't run." It's only partly a show. He's exaggerating his job to make theirs seem easier, but he really does hate the damn thing, the way he hates his own helplessness. It's like everything today.

Peeling back the tarp, he's almost hoping the gas tank's dry. The snowblower's old, the faded red of farm machinery, dirty bicycle grips with twin hand clutches for forward and reverse and blade speed, as well as a separate throttle and choke. Tiny cotton balls of spider's eggs dot the webs around the plug wires. He can't remember the last time he used it—March, April, back when he and Jacquie were together and the days were a blur—or putting it away, but he must have. Even then, in that careless (and, he'd thought, endless) trance, he wouldn't have left it empty. He unscrews the metal cap and tips his head to one side until light glints in the still liquid the color of ginger ale. Impossible to tell how deep or shallow. Half full, maybe. Enough.

He backs it out. The dusty tires are soft.

"You can do it!" Ty says, in a hearty Rob Schneider.

"I-I-I—I will try, Coach," Manny answers, and thinks at least they're making fun of him to his face.

There's no reason not to wear the jacket now (he checks on his tie, still damp), yet he hesitates before drawing it on, then idiotically zips up the front. Like a mother, Roz offers him her gloves—too small; he doesn't want to stretch them out. Jacquie watches him use his ass to back through the swinging door, and while it makes no sense, he wonders, half hoping it's true, if she could possibly be jealous, or hurt. He's not going to apologize for a phone call, or for Deena. He and Jacquie haven't talked about the baby beyond a strained congratulations, as if it's none of her business, and maybe it isn't, not now.

Outside, the walk is a trough between foot-high banks, the only trace of footprints his own—surprising, way more duck-footed than he'd believe, making him immediately straighten his toes. The neon above the front door tints everything a heat-lamp pink, including the chipped instruction decal between the choke and the throttle. After all these years he should know the starting sequence by heart, but even before he finishes reading the six steps, his brain rejects them as a whole. Simpler to turn the crank that positions the chute that throws the snow, curved like a periscope.

There's no point in stalling. Even if he doesn't believe the instructions, no one's going to come rescue him.

Patiently, precisely, he follows the steps, daring them to work.

Set transmission level to engage. Turn fuel knob to on. Pull choke out. Set throttle to fast (the running rabbit symbol). Pull starter cord. Push choke in.

His first try, he never gets to 'push choke in.' The starter cord is balky, having sat curled tight for eight months. He yanks the plastic handle, feeling the muscles in his shoulder pull away from the bones, until the rotor inside finally turns, a tinny spinning that rattles and slows, stops without ignition.

His third try is better, the rotor jangling, but nowhere close to turning over. Again, and nothing. Again.

"Don't fucking do this," he says, and rechecks the settings: engage, on, choke out, rabbit. "Right."

He squeezes the handle tight, takes a deep breath and hauls back hard. The rotor whizzes, the motor catches, just a cough, and dies. He does it again and nothing happens.

"What the fuck."

He looks up past the haze of lights to the sky for patience but finds only clouds, more snow dropping straight as rain.

"Come on."

Again. Again. Again. Again.

His patience is finished. Now it's simply him setting his feet, leaning back and tugging the fucking cord over and over. It's freezing but he's beginning to sweat, beads catching in his eyebrows, and by the time the engine putts and pops to life, sputtering blue smoke that floats away over the drifted benches, his chin is wet, and the back of his neck, and he's panting out hot clouds of his own.

He remembers to push the choke in, and it stops.

"Fuckin' piece of shit."

The next time, he gets it. He flicks sweat from his forehead and waves the flaps of his jacket, letting the engine run until it's steady before squeezing the clutch that sets the blades spinning.

He guides the machine up and down the main walk, plodding along behind like he's mowing a lawn, using the crank to turn the chute at the end so it doesn't vomit the chopped snow back on a clean spot. Now that it's actually working, he's amazed how big of a difference it makes, eating down to the bare concrete. If it doesn't snow any harder than it is, and he gets some ice melter down, one pass could do it. The lot's not perfect, but with the walk clear, he can make a better case for staying open. Okay, so he must be officially desperate, he thinks, for the snowblower to be his friend.

He does the wing toward the mall first, afraid he'll run out of gas. He can't remember the last time it was serviced, but the engine is racketing, and he wonders—as he wonders about the marlin, and the live lobsters— where it will end up. After his abuelita died, he had to clear out the house, and since he knew he was moving to an apartment, he sold her clattering old Lawnboy at a weekend-long yard sale. It's in some Salvadoran family's garage, waiting for spring, or so he hopes, and not cannibalized for parts.

Following along, blinking and sniffling, shuffling to keep up, he thinks that may have been why he fell for Jacquie. Losing his grandmother and the only home he'd known, he needed something to cling to. But then, why not Deena? Why not Deena now?

That's the question he can't answer, just as he can't say exactly what he feels for her, or what future they may have together, and he thinks with a sudden weariness that he doesn't love her enough, and probably never will, and that later they'll both have to pay for this fault of his, more than he and Jacquie already have.

It's too easy to think outside, by himself, and he wishes he had his iPod, Café Tacuba grooving (but even they might lead him in the wrong direction today, the wrong car, the wrong room, the wrong bed).

Dom's gone, just Roz's CRV stranded out there by itself, drifted to the hubs. The gas is going to last, except he's cold now, finishing the far wing (where no one will ever set foot, he thinks), and hungry from skipping lunch, a headache tightening his sinuses. Still, he wants to do a good job and doesn't cheat, edging the curb perfectly. He's not coming out here again unless he absolutely has to.

Spreading the ice melter, he notices his right arm is shaking. His fingers are numb and then tingly, cramped from fighting the vibration. Inside, putting the snowblower away, the cover keeps slipping out of his grip, and even after he rubs and flexes them, his hands feel weak.

The kitchen is quiet besides the radio. Ty and Rich and Leron are arranging their chafing dishes by the hot plate as if to show him they're all done.

"Lemme have the usual," he orders.

Ty's surprised, it's so late, but for just a second, and does an about-face.

"What's the vegetable?"

"Cauliflower."

"That was lunch."

"Okay—albino broccoli."

"Make that no vegetable."

Manny goes to the bar and pours himself a Diet Coke with lemon, then has to pick it up with both hands. The UConn game is over and the new game is close to halftime. On the other TV, the Weather Channel is showing exactly what it showed three hours ago, and he reaches up and changes to Channel 30, right down the road from them, and gets the national news, video of shoppers milling around malls—the usual story about retailers counting on the Christmas season, as if the economy is solely dependent on the holidays. The other local channels tell him nothing, so he settles for ESPN with the sound turned down and stands there sipping. The teams mean nothing to him, and by the first commercial he's paying more attention to the liquor bottles tiered three deep across the mirror, worried that his inventory won't match. Even wholesale, a fifth of Chivas costs a lot, and while the amount won't be held against his check, if he wants his own place again, Manny needs to show headquarters he can manage his resources. After the Lobster's performance, he can't afford much spillage.

He keys on the top shelf of scotches, the colors designed to draw the eye like fine wood. The Chivas is almost full, but he doesn't remember the Crown Royal being so low, and he'd swear he just replaced that Dewar's, down to a couple fingers. Yes, this morning, because Dom was late. Before he can investigate, Roz calls from the break room that his dinner's ready.

He can't quite rid himself of the suspicion as he eats, pulling a stool up to the far end of the table, way down by the Frialators (he has to get his own napkin and silverware, and from habit sets himself a place). The fear, of course, isn't that Dom's pouring himself drinks but stealing whole bottles—open, for his own consumption, or sealed, for resale. A few years ago they had a problem with a summer replacement hiding wine in empty boxes behind the dumpster. Manny has no reason to think Dom has been anything but solid, but strange things happen when people know it's the last day, as if the rules have been suspended.

He frowns over Ty's scampi, plated as if for a critic, the headless necks of the shrimp pointed toward the center of the dish, bodies arranged in a symmetric swirl, tails overlapped around the edge counterclockwise, parsley flakes for garnish. It's the chain's most popular dish, simple, and horribly boring for any real chef. Ty's been making it for Manny nearly ten years, and tonight it's as fine as ever, the garlic biting through the buttery richness, a breathless hint of white wine to finish. The pilaf is fluffed and light, not wet and heavy as he's had at other Lobsters. It's not Ty's fault they're closing—but Ty knows this; Ty would never doubt himself. And it's not their last scampi either: It's on the Olive Garden's permanent menu.

Ty's farther up the table on his own stool, chewing a toothpick and leafing through an old *Old Car Trader*.

"Chieftain," Manny says to get his attention, then waggles his hand palm down to show it's only so-so, earning him a quick finger.

The deejays change at six, the new guy making a big deal of how long it took him to drive in, telling everyone to avoid the roads if they don't absolutely have to be out, advice Manny silently rejects. This is the beginning of the Lobster's volume hours. Now he wonders if their numbers were hurt not only by the construction on 9 but all the snow last winter. He tells himself he's giving up the guest count (sixty-one, pathetic for a Saturday, honestly not worth opening for).

In the corner by the dishwasher, Rich and Leron are playing a form of horse with the dead biscuits from lunch, using the garbage can as a basket. When Manny's finished, Rich comes over and takes his plate, sliding it expertly down the counter to Leron, who blasts it with the sprayer and racks it so they can get back to their game.

Roz and Jacquie have settled into the break room— Roz smoking, using her coffee saucer as an ashtray. She's complaining about her middle daughter bringing her boyfriend home for Christmas. This is the daughter in Florida who got in a bad car accident, stopped drinking and found religion. The boyfriend's part of the church and twenty years older. "I don't know," Roz says, "he's nice, but he's nice *all the time*. It's kinda creepy."

"That is kinda weird," Manny says.

"You don't know," Jacquie says. "Maybe she needs that right now."

"Well, I don't," Roz says. "It's my vacation too. I don't need Jesus ruining it for me. How 'bout you, you going anywhere?"

"I might go down to the city for a couple days. Depends on what I get."

Manny can counter with Bridgeport, but doesn't, imagining Jacquie at Rockefeller Center (not Rodney, just Jacquie), watching the skaters circle under that funky gold statue of the guy lying on his side and the big tree with the GE building behind it, where they make *Saturday Night Live*. His abuelita took him once when he was little; he still remembers the flags and the glass elevator that went down into the ground. He wanted to skate, but the line was too long, and he didn't know how anyway.

"Hey," Roz asks him, "you making the lunch schedule next month?"

"No one's talked to me about it, so I'm going to say no."

"So where all are you looking?" Roz asks Jacquie.

He'd meant to just breeze through, and now, standing there while they're sitting, he feels like an intruder on their conversation. No one's manning the host stand, and he uses it as an excuse, ducking through the swinging door into the empty dining room, where the candles waver on the tables and Marvin Gaye and Tammi Terrell are harmonizing—"Ain't nothing like the real thing, baby." The lights blink around the live tank, the tinsel and the marlin's belly echoing their colors. Outside, the walk is still pretty bare, just a downy layer he can see through, and while the odds are against it, Manny takes some minor satisfaction in knowing that they're ready if somebody comes.

No one does, giving him time to miss Eddie (he still has his Powerball tickets—or ticket) and to fret over whether Dom snuck anything out while he was in the mall. He paces the main room and back into the foyer, glancing out at the parking lot, rehearsing what he might say to Jacquie if he gets the chance to be alone with her. Every pair of headlights could be Rodney, come to take her away forever, unless he does something, but what can he do or say that he hasn't tried already?

The worst thing is that at heart he knows she's right, that what he wanted was childish and impossible, and that he was lucky just to have her for even a little while. He's never seen himself as the kind of person who'd throw away everything for an entirely new life, and that's what both of them would have had to do. Jacquie understood that—from the beginning, it seems, so that throughout their time together she had to remind him this was just temporary, even when she wanted to believe in it herself. For once in his life he was the dreamer, forcing her to be the responsible one, and naturally she resented it, attacking him when they should have been happiest, confusing him, making him think their problems were all his fault when he was willing to give up anything to be with her. Now he realizes how crazy that sounds—and how cruel, with the baby on the way and Deena relying on him—but he'd really believed it then, and would have gone through with it if Jacquie hadn't thought it all out for both of them. And while she was right—is right—

sometimes he wishes she hadn't. Sometimes, selfishly, he wishes she was so lost in him she wouldn't have been able to save them from doing something stupid.

Turning in to the hall, he comes across a scarf left on top of the coatrack—black, knitted and soft, with a tag from Nordstrom's (not a bad gift, he thinks). Probably belongs to someone from the retirement party. In back they have a box that serves as a lost & found. Manny parades the scarf by Roz and Jacquie before adding it to the two Totes umbrellas and the sweat-stained Yankee cap and dirty plastic rattle, even though tomorrow they'll probably chuck the whole thing.

Above the box his tie hangs over the rod, still damp but close enough to dry that he takes it to the bathroom and holds it under the blower for a couple of cycles, then puts it on hot, fixing the length in the mirror. In the massive handicapped stall he flips it over his shoulder before he sits, then waits, staring at the black-and-white tiles between his feet, the rare red one tossed in as an accent. He's linking them together like a word search, his thighs going numb, when the bathroom door thumps and then squeaks open, letting in a gush of Celine Dion.

"Hey boss," Roz calls.

"Yeah?"

"Get off the pot. We got customers."

Pulling the cheap toilet paper gently so it won't rip, his

first thought is a daydream so stale he automatically fast-forwards through it. The car creeping across the lot is full of robbers or terrorists taking advantage of the bad weather to lay siege to the place. They take everyone else hostage while Manny hides in the men's room, ultimately sneaking out and saving the Lobster by his guts and wits like Bruce Willis in *Die Hard*.

In reality, the customers are a frail old couple who have no business being out in this weather. The woman totters up the walk, the husband leading to one side like an orderly, both hands clamped around her arm to steady her, and still she lurches and wobbles as if she'll topple over. Manny goes out in the cold and holds the door for them, and has to restrain himself from doing more. He thinks they're just leaning into the wind, but as they pass he sees they're both hunched, the woman slope-shouldered, the man actually hunchbacked, his shoulders up around his ears.

Inside, the man helps the woman off with her coat and nearly pulls her over backwards. Manny sticks close, ready to catch them—a different kind of hero.

"You folks traveling?" he asks, slipping two dinner menus from the holder on the side of the host stand as if it's natural for the restaurant to be completely deserted.

"I guess you could call it that," the man says loudly, as if still in the storm. "We were s'posed to be home by now."

"It's bad out," Manny agrees, and leads them into the dining room, giving them a window booth with a view of their car, a new Lincoln. As he leans in to set their menus down, he catches a piercing loop of feedback like the wow of a distant late-night radio station and realizes it's coming from the man's hearing aid. In the lamplight, the man's hands are swollen, a black and gold Masonic ring cutting into one finger. The woman puts her whole face into the menu, tilting one eye close to the print. On her wrists she has grape-colored bruises and blotchy, paper-thin skin like his abuelita that last year, and reflexively Manny wonders what the man will do when she's gone.

"What's the soup?" the man asks.

Manny adjusts his own volume. "New England clam chowder and Bayou seafood gumbo."

"I mean the soup of the day."

"We don't have a specialty soup today, I'm afraid."

"Huh," the man says, as if he's been cheated.

"What?" the woman says.

"There's no soup of the day."

"Well that's a pity, isn't it?"

Manny assures them a server will be out with some hot Cheddar Bay biscuits for them in just a minute.

Technically it's Roz's section, but they flipped a coin and Jacquie lost.

"I figure she'd want to take one last one for old time's sake. Plus she can use the money more than I can."

"Yeah, thanks," Jacquie says. "He looks like a big tipper."

It may not be a big table for Jacquie, but Manny has to squash the urge to hover and retreats to the kitchen, where Ty is still bent over the *Old Car Trader,* admiring Corvettes.

"Check this out," Ty says, pointing to a Stingray convertible from the midsixties that costs almost double what the bank wanted for his grandmother's house.

"We've got cottonheads."

"I heard."

Jacquie swings in. "Two broiled flounder, one baked, one rice."

"That was fast," Manny says.

"They're hungry. It's almost their bedtime."

"No flounder," Ty says, tipping the page.

"Haddock?" Jacquie circles, stopping at the coffee urn.

"Tilapia."

"You're going to make me sell them tilapia."

"Can't sell what you ain't got."

"You need drinks?" Manny asks.

"Got 'em." And she's gone.

Manny wants to follow and apologize, table touch with the old folks to let them know they're not always this poorly stocked, as if he wants their return business. He has to content himself with getting their salads, choosing the best two, tossing out a white spine of lettuce. He microwaves an extra set of biscuits, just in case.

When Jacquie returns, everyone waits for her order. She crosses all the way to the hot plate.

"So?" Ty has to ask.

"So tilapia."

"Thass my girl."

The line kicks into gear, Rich and Leron taking their stations. With such a small order, they've got it covered, and rather than watch them, Manny rolls around front and mans the host stand as if he's expecting the usual dinner rush. Outside, the snow falls steadily, endlessly. The couple hunch over their salads, the woman losing a few pieces of lettuce off her fork, gathering them back to her plate with her hand. Jacquie has just delivered their second set of biscuits when the lights dim and blink, making everyone, including Manny, look up.

Kool & the Gang stop celebrating in midchorus. The lamps and overheads flicker, and the string around the live tank, the shaded tube on the host stand. All of them go dark at once, then pop on, surging even brighter, to fade again, swelling, cycling as if trying to find the right balance, a tease, finally dying and staying off, leaving only the candles mirrored in the windows and a strange quiet.

"It's all right," Manny broadcasts, just as the emergency lighting clicks on—a battery-powered box on the far wall that throws more shadow than light.

He goes over and reassures the couple that this is merely temporary, not a problem at all. And it shouldn't be: The grill should still work, and the furnace, and the water. He jokes that with the snow and the power failure, they're having some kind of adventure.

"I'm sorry, but I can't see a thing," the woman says, setting down her fork and leaning back as if she's quitting.

"Hold on," Manny says like he has an idea, and with Jacquie moves candles from the neighboring tables until their faces glow.

"Very romantic," Jacquie shills, though from Manny's vantage point, recalling the last time he saw her skin softened by this rich light, she doesn't have to.

The man breaks a biscuit in half and butters it. The woman bends and picks up her fork again.

In the kitchen Roz is setting out candles while Ty plates the tilapia. He shoos Leron and Rich; it's easier to do all the garnishing himself. Manny's glad to see he's serious, lining up his three best lemon slices like a stoplight down the center of the fillet, plucking a stray grain of rice from the rim. This could be the last meal they serve, and like everything today, he wants it to be perfect.

He hangs back as Jacquie takes the tray out. It's only seven twenty but with the darkness it feels later. Any other night Manny would be calculating his pars for tomorrow and placing his produce order. Instead, he leans out the back door and smokes, looking up at the blackness over the trees behind the dumpster, where there should be the glow of their neon sign by the highway. No one can see them, so no one knows they're open. There's no better argument for closing, and nothing Manny can do but hope power comes back on soon. For now he just flicks his filter into the snow and shuts the door.

He crunches a mint before his table touch, pinching the tips of his collar to make sure they're buttoned—silly, since the couple probably couldn't see them even if the lights were on.

"Don't worry, you look great," Roz says, not pausing her game of solitaire.

After the break room, lit by a single candle, the dining room seems bright—and warm, the flames producing the illusion of heat. Manny glides by their booth as if he's on his way somewhere else and finds them tearing into their tilapia like it was flounder.

"How is everything tonight?"

"Good," the man says.

The woman just nods, chewing.

Manny wants more—wants them to say this is the best meal they've ever eaten, and the most memorable; wants the man to shake his hand and tell him he's done a great job under tough circumstances—but that's all they're going to give him.

"Anything else I can get for you folks? More coffee?"

"No thanks."

"Okay," Manny says. "Enjoy your dinner."

They're eating, so he should be satisfied. Any other day that would be enough. It's unfair of him to expect everyone to feel what he's feeling, whether it's justified or not.

Sixty-three guests, that makes. Any normal Saturday the restaurant would be packed by now, the overflow waiting with pagers, clogging the bar and the foyer, sucking down beers and Lobsteritas, Manny running around trying to help everybody at once. With nothing to do, he doesn't know how to kill the time, and ends up bugging Roz for a while and then spying on the old couple, watching them finish, then clearing for Jacquie. He thinks he's inordinately proud that they both cleaned their plates.

The machine is down, so Leron does the dishes by hand in the big sink, Rich drying for him. Manny doesn't bug them about the minimum rinse temperature; whoever gets the dishes will just have to run them again anyway.

The old folks don't want dessert, no surprise. Without a POS to process the check, Jacquie has to write up a paper ticket. Manny totals it, digging a calculator out of the host stand drawer to do the tax, and then the man hands Jacquie his American Express.

It's up to Manny to ask if he has cash.

"I've got some," the man says, "but I'd rather hang on to it. We've still got to get to Springfield."

The charitable solution here is to take down the man's credit card number and have him sign the bill, then trace over his signature when they get power back. It's simple to do, but the day's been so crazy that it seems pointlessly complicated to Manny, especially when they're the only customers, and more out of impatience than anything else, he makes a command decision. It may look bad on the End of Day, especially after the numbers they've put up, and him comping dinner for the staff, but it seems only fitting that their last meal should be on the house.

After a brief show of protest from the husband, the offer produces the gush and the handshake Manny wanted from his table touch.

"I'll tell you," the man says, counting out a generous tip for Jacquie, "that is the best thing that's happened to us all day, and it's been a long one."

"Now I wish I'd ordered dessert," the woman says.

Manny can't let them navigate the sloppy walk in the dark by themselves, and enlists Jacquie's help. He's not sure driving's such a good idea, but the man's determined, saying they've made it this far. It's only another forty or so miles. The road's open, it's just slow going.

Outside, the mall has vanished, the only lights those of passing cars on the highway. The plows are out, but still Manny's glad they've got the Lincoln with its massive hood. He and Jacquie help them in, then stand there in the headlights, waving them away like relatives. Manny thinks they'll turn the wrong way at the light, but no, they make the right toward 9.

He finds Jacquie looking at him. "What are you doing?"

"What do you mean?" he asks.

"You've been acting weird all day."

"It's been a weird day."

"I mean around me. One minute you want me to come to the Olive Garden with you, then you don't say five words to me the rest of the day. Are you mad at me or something? Because I didn't do anything. Didn't we say this was the best thing? For me *and* for you. For everybody. Right?"

He's aware, more than ever, of the Zales box in his pocket. He could go down on one knee in the snow and give her Deena's earrings and it wouldn't change a thing, so why is he tempted? Because he doesn't know what to say. Easier to make a big gesture, even if it's not the right one, than to explain himself.

"Not everybody," he says.

She slaps him backhand in the chest, and not playfully. "You promised you wouldn't do this, so don't, okay?"

"I just don't know what I'm going to do, you know."

"You'll do what everyone does."

"What's that?"

"You'll have your baby and get married and buy a house somewhere."

"I don't know about that."

"That's what you're going to do, and you'll be happy, mowing your lawn every weekend, making sure everything's perfect. I know you, Manny. That's what you want."

"We could have done that." It's unfair of him. This isn't how he wants to say good-bye.

Jacquie just shakes her head, and he feels foolish for ever hoping she'd want to be with him—as if he was too stupid all along to see what was obvious to everyone else from the beginning.

"Come on," she says, trying to soothe him. "Remember that time we went to the park and went wading in the creek and saw those fish?"

"Yeah."

"That's what I wanted. And we were lucky. We had that."

"I still want that."

"You think I don't? I'd love to have that again with you, Manny, but it's not possible. And we both know it's not right."

Rodney, she means, and now Deena, and the baby. Her life and his, the complications he conveniently forgets. He's always known it was wrong, yet he wants to argue with her—things change, they can do anything they want—but knows she'll only get mad at him, as if he doesn't understand. Maybe he's just being stubborn.

They agreed this would be the easiest way; at times he's felt guilty about how convenient it is, walking away clean. Now he's not even sure what that means.

"You make me think too much," he says, then shrugs. "I actually like that about you."

"I don't know why," Jacquie says.

"I don't know either." And he's not just saying this. It's true: He's still not sure exactly what happened. She was beautiful and smart and funny, and that was when he didn't even know her.

She turns, a cue for him to turn too. He wants to make a final declaration out here in the dark before they rejoin the others—"I love you" or something equally futile—but she's already headed for the door, escaping him again, as always.

Inside, everyone has gathered around a low table in the bar, as if the night is over. Rich and Leron lounge in soft chairs with their feet up, still wearing their aprons. Manny and Jacquie split, out of habit taking seats on opposite sides of the group. Roz has her shoes off and is telling about the time Fat Kathy's ex-boyfriend got arrested for fighting with her in the parking lot. Manny's heard her tell the story before and reclines in the candlelight, only half listening, anticipating the punchline: Fat Kathy cursing out Manny for calling the cops because she wasn't done kicking the guy's ass (untrue on almost all counts: Manny didn't call them, Joanne did, after the guy split

Fat Kathy's nose open; Fat Kathy only said that last part as a joke on herself, holding a rag to her face). That was a long time ago, before Jacquie started, another lifetime. But this is too, just as separate, as if none of it's connected. Sitting in the dark, he flashes on him and Jacquie in his car by the dumpster, even though they were careful never to make out in the parking lot. They liked going to the park, sitting at the picnic tables by the creek behind the stadium, leaning over the rail of the footbridge and watching the twigs they dropped float downstream.

"Manny," Roz is saying.

"What?"

"What was his name? Boyd, Burt, Bart—something country."

"Bret."

"So Bret's been sitting in his truck sipping Jack and thinking," she goes on. Manny closes his eyes a second, trying to recall the guy's face. He can see his truck, a big square Chevy, a red flannel shirt, maybe a beard. He remembers Fat Kathy in uniform, complete with her nametag, as if she might pull a shift, but the boyfriend's gone, and he thinks that's how he'll be to Rodney, a fat, faceless name with a big key ring, Jacquie's old boss. And that's good, that's how it should be.

After the punchline gets a mild laugh, Roz turns to Leron and says, "How'd you get that mouse, anyway?"

Leron stares at her, slit-eyed and silent, as if she has no

right. For a second Manny's afraid he'll go off on her, or just not answer. Leron tilts his head and touches a finger to his cheek. "Some cat gave it to me."

"Ow," Ty says, wincing.

Suzanne gets the treatment next. Everyone knows her, so they all pile on. Even Manny has to laugh at the time she told someone on the host-stand phone to fuck off with a party standing right there.

"That girl was evil," Ty says.

"You didn't have to deal with her," Jacquie says. "Remember the time she triple-sat Nicolette—"

"While Le Ly's section was completely empty," Roz says.

"That's another one I don't know why you hired," Ty says.

Which starts them on Joe, who only ate tater tots and broke the big mixer by jamming it with the paddle, and Danny, who used to park his primered Integra next to Ty's Supra, and Marisol, who got pregnant and threw up in the hygiene sink, and Kaylie, who sang for an Irish band they all went and saw one drunken Friday after hours. Roz remembers the years when they had their own softball team and adopt-a-highway mile on 9, and while Manny was working then, it seems like they're talking about a whole other place. The feeling was different, and it wasn't just Jacquie. He was in charge the entire time, yet he can't figure out how they got from there to here. Their numbers weren't that bad.

Ramon P., who could spin on his head, and Frankie, with his wrist and ankle weights, and Des, and Santos, and Michelle, and J.T. The day the ice maker broke and flooded the stockroom. The guy, not that old, who had a heart attack in the bathroom.

"Thanks," Manny says, "I almost forgot about him."

A cell phone goes off—not his but a bumping Missy ringtone, "Get Ur Freak On": Jacquie's. She leaves the bar to answer it, and he thinks it must be Rodney. He still owes Deena a call—they need to talk about tomorrow. He should just shut it down and let everyone go home. Instead, he sits there in the dark, listening to his own history, waiting for Jacquie to come back, but when she does she sits down without a word, and the days when he could ask her who it was are over.

Unconsciously he counters, taking out his own phone to see if he has any messages. When he flips it open, the lights snap on above the table, making them shield their eyes like vampires.

They wait, squinting, as if this might just be temporary. The TVs natter, the live tank burbles, the colored string blinks. The only thing missing is the house music. Manny gets up and goes to the front doors. The walk is frosted red, red flakes falling softly. The mall's back, and the stoplight, and when he cuts through the empty kitchen and stands on the loading dock he can see the glow of their sign by the highway.

"Looks like we're back in business," he announces, trying to hide his excitement.

The group's already breaking up, dragging back to their stations as if more guests are on the way, and now Manny misses them all sitting together in the dark. He turns the house music on again, takes the host stand and waits. It's strange being the only one up front, or maybe he's just tired, finishing the long double shift. Jacquie hasn't asked him if she can leave early, so that's good. He checks his phone: No new messages. He's lectured every greeter about keeping theirs off; now he ignores his own policy, watching the road from the front doors before dialing.

"Hey, babe," Deena says, with the TV on behind her. She's probably in bed already. She's been going to sleep earlier and earlier, and then tosses all night, waking him. It's another reason he's been staying at his place.

"You called me?"

"I just wanted to see what's up with tomorrow."

"I gotta be here from eleven till two."

Voices crisscross in the background. She laughs, then silence, as if she's stopped listening to him.

"What are you watching?"

"That movie with Bill Murray where he's supposed to be Scrooge."

"Scrooged," Manny says.

"It's pretty funny," she says, as if she didn't expect it to be. "So what time are you getting here?"

"I don't know. Four, four thirty?" He's wandered over to the marlin, inspecting its glass eye, shaving the dust off the top with the side of his thumb.

"It doesn't take two hours to get here."

"I want to change."

"You can change here. Bring a bag with you. It's just dinner. It's not like you're staying overnight."

This is an old argument, and Manny knows to leave it alone. "Three thirty," he says, keeping a half hour for himself.

"What are you wearing? You need to look nice for Mami."

"I don't know. What I usually wear."

"No. Wear your blue shirt."

"It's not ironed."

"Bring it. I'll iron it for you."

Deena wants to talk about their plans for New Year's—already set, he'd thought. "I can't drink, so I'll drive," she's saying. He moves to the live tank, peering down at the last survivors, their claws banded yellow, the blinking lights turning them carnival colors. He thought he'd done a decent job of managing them, but now he sees he was optimistic. Even if it hadn't snowed, he wouldn't have sold them all in a single night.

"... and then we'll go back to my place," Deena says. "Does that sound good?"

"Sure," he says, and shifts to the front doors again, gazing out at the lot, his breath fogging the glass. She's laughing at Bill Murray again, and he has nothing to say. He wants to believe it's because of the day, or because he's tired.

"Okay," he says, "so, four."

"Three thirty."

"Right, I'll see you tomorrow."

As they dawdle, a police car glides silently along the highway with its lights flashing. Following as if being escorted is a tall bus, the fancy kind people take to the casinos. He and Deena finally say good-bye as the cop car slows and stops at the light for the mall. The bus pulls in right behind it, signaling left. Manny keeps his eye on them, the phone still open in his hand. The mall's open late for the holidays, but no one goes to the mall in a bus like that, not the Willow Brook Mall. He disconnects, then makes sure to turn the phone off, watching the cop turn in and then up the access road, heading straight for them. He wants to yell to the break room, but waits, needing to be certain, as the cop signals and turns into the lot, then the bus. Manny runs.

And almost bowls over Jacquie as he bursts through the door. "We got a bus."

And into the kitchen. "We got a bus."

"You gotta be fucking kidding me," Ty says, not moving from his stool.

"I'm not kidding. Let's go." He claps like a coach. "Everybody on the line, right now."

He circles around front, ready to see the cop and the bus leaving, but here comes a trooper through the snow like a scout. Manny opens the door of the vestibule to meet him.

"You guys open?" the trooper asks.

Out of habit—or is it pride?—Manny says "Till eleven," and points to the plaque with their hours.

"Mind if these folks use your restrooms?"

"Not at all."

"Thanks." He steps outside and waves to the bus driver to send them in. "Tour group ate at this place in Waterbury and got some bad mussels. Lot of them are older folks, so we're trying to take every precaution. Got any bottled water?"

"Perrier, that's it."

"Bubbles in that?"

"Yep."

"How about just regular water?"

"I can give them ice water in glasses."

"That would be great. How big are your restrooms—how many stalls?"

"Four and two. Four in the women's."

"That'll do. Driver was trying to get by with just the one lavatory on the bus. Not a happy situation."

"Ours are clean," Manny says, but now he wishes he'd hit them again after lunch.

The first passengers come in bent over, holding themselves against the cold. Manny's surprised to find they're all Chinese. He directs them down the hall, then goes in back and explains the situation to the crew, asking Jacquie and Roz to run two trays of ice water and set them on jacks in the foyer.

"So no one's eating anything," Ty asks, "is that right? They're just off-loading."

"They already ate and it didn't work."

"Well, that is fucking disappointing. Is he going to look at my windshield?"

"He's not really here to do that."

"Don't cost nothing to ask."

Manny doesn't, of course. He stands by in case they need more paper towels, offering water to the passengers, who don't seem to speak any English. They pass around small plastic tubes like crack vials, dumping out what look like peppercorns, some sort of herbal remedy. The old women are tiny, and remind him of his abuelita, frail and at the mercy of another language. He bows, gesturing to the goblets with an open hand, but hardly anyone takes one. It's only when another passenger takes his place, instructing the others, that they gradually empty the trays, standing around in groups like some bizarre cocktail party. Manny's about to ask Roz and Jacquie to restock when the driver—a bony man with crooked dentures—asks everyone to please reboard the bus, or at least that's how Manny translates it, because they all set their glasses back on the trays and follow him out. A few thank Manny in their way, and he smiles and nods back.

He has Jacquie check the women's room to make sure they're all out, while he checks the men's. It's no dirtier than usual, the sink wet, some slushy footprints, a single gauzy square of toilet paper on the floor of a stall.

The trooper's waiting for him at the front doors, and gives the driver the thumbs-up. Manny doesn't ask him why he doesn't escort them back to 9. He's more interested in why he chose the Lobster in the first place.

The trooper points toward the sky. "Sign said BUSES WELCOME."

"They are," Manny says, and once he's gone, estimates how many passengers they served and adds sixty to the guest count—over a hundred and twenty now, not the worst day they've had.

When he checks in on the kitchen, Leron and Rich are racking the water goblets. The back door's open to bleed off the heat, and Ty's outside, clearing his windshield while his car idles, the defroster on high. He's already cleaned Manny's.

Since he's out here anyway, Manny can't resist a peek at the dumpster, swinging the gates open to scare the rats. The light above casts a metallic glare, but the fence has slats that throw deep shadows. The footprints in the snow along the far side are bigger than his, and when he turns the corner, there on the ground, the lid covered with a couple of inches, is an uncrushed Smirnoff box. Inside he finds a haul: three almost-full bottles of Cuervo, Tanqueray and Hennessy. He should have never gone to the mall.

He takes the bottles and leaves the box.

"Someone leave you a present?" Ty asks.

"Someone."

"Dumb one." Because he's never gotten along with Dom.

"Probably."

He makes sure Rich is occupied on the ass end of the dishwasher before slipping in and stashing the bottles in the stockroom. Now that they've been outside, he can't safely put them back, even if he believes there's nothing wrong with them (they're already spillage, the cost automatically charged against his inventory), but it seems a shame that they'll go to waste. Maybe a thank-you for Leron and Rich, assuming they weren't the ones who boosted them.

That can wait. First he needs to clean the bathrooms— not in case someone comes, but because he can't stand a job left undone. He could delegate it and no one would complain (not to his face), but right now Manny needs something to concentrate on, and he's always loved the perfection of a clean mirror, the visible progress of mopping.

When he finishes, it's twenty past ten. The night's almost over. Only a fool would expect someone to show up now, and he doesn't want to keep his people a minute longer than he absolutely has to. Technically they'll still be open till eleven. One by one, he's given up whatever goals he'd hoped to achieve today, so even though the decision's obvious, he has to tell himself he's not really quitting.

He asks Jacquie and Roz to come into the kitchen with him so they can all hear it at the same time.

"That's it," he announces. "Let's shut it down."

END OF DAY

Everything gets tossed. The skewers, the fries, the rice—anything they stockpiled. The coleslaw goes, and the baked potatoes, all the cauliflower, tray on tray of biscuits. Normally they'd save the chowder and gumbo. With oven mitts he delivers the pots to Leron, who dumps them steaming into the gurgling InSinkErator. The waste, Manny thinks, imagining how many people a soup kitchen downtown could feed with this. Any vegetables they cut. Any sauces they prepared today. He rolls the garbage can over to the reach-in and clears the shelves. The garnishes at the hot plate in their little chafing dishes—the lemon slices and chopped parsley and Parmesan cheese and sour cream.

"Chuck it in a bucket," Ty says, handing Rich a saucepan of herb butter.

"What have you done with Ty?" Manny asks, mock-horrified, because usually by this time of night he's enjoying his chef's privilege of sitting on his stool and watching the others clean up.

"I'm like Troy Brown—I'm all about the team."

"So I guess that makes me Bill Belichick."

"No, you Romeo Crennel," Ty says, which gets a laugh, because he's fat.

"Who they playin' tomorrow?" Rich asks.

It's just grab-ass chatter, a way to keep things moving, but Manny can't help but remember all the playoff games and Super Bowls they rented a big-screen TV for, the thousand-dollar pools they taped up behind the bar (against company policy, and nervous-making for him). When the Patriots won that first time, on the final play, he and Eddie hugged so hard he almost chipped a tooth.

Ty has the kitchen under control, so he goes out front and deals with the bar. There's no need to restock, yet his eyes are automatically drawn to any bottles that are low, his mind making a list he immediately wipes clean. He locks the coolers and the bar back. The liquor stays, but any open mixers like the grapefruit juice go straight down the drain. He pitches the olives and cocktail onions, the lemon and lime wedges, the orange and pineapple slices, the maraschino cherries and strawberries. The plate of margarita salt crusted in circles—gone. He runs a pitcher each of frozen margaritas and Bahama Mamas before draining the machines, figuring someone might like one while they watch the Powerball drawing. While he's thinking of it, he switches both TVs to Channel 6.

In the dining room, Jacquie and Roz are using carts to clear the tables, stacking appetizer dishes and collecting bundles of silverware and the tea lights and the damned stand-up drink-and-dessert menus he could never keep clean—tearing down this morning's setup in reverse. Manny can't imagine corporate would try to recycle the salt and pepper, but he'll let the bean counters deal with that. The same for the Lobster swizzle sticks and coasters and napkins, though they're probably unsanitary.

With a pang, he realizes he could have saved the chowder and gumbo (or at least the chowder) and given it away to any customers who show up tomorrow, along with the gift certificates.

"Hey," Roz hollers from halfway across the dining room, pointing to the ceiling, "can I turn the muzak off? I swear, if I hear 'This One's for the Girls' one more time, I'm seriously gonna kill somebody."

"Go ahead," Manny says. "I mean go ahead and turn it off." So now there's just the TVs, the back half of the ten o'clock news nattering as he wipes down the cutting boards and rinses the little sink.

The bathrooms are clean, and he takes care of the worst of the foyer and the hall carpet with the push sweeper. He can vacuum the dining room in the morning—but see, he's thinking like it's any other night. There's no point vacuuming, or even sweeping up, because they're going to tear the place apart. Just as there's probably no point worrying about his inventory. He's already been demoted.

The coatrack's empty, and the host stand's squared away, the staff schedule for tomorrow blank. As a tribute, he leaves today's specials on the chalkboard. He boxes the mismatched ornaments in their nests of brittle tissue paper and unplugs the string of lights, coiling it around his elbow like a roadie. The tinsel he pitches.

"Hey," Jacquie says, "what are the lobsters supposed to look at now?"

"Each other," Manny says, and a shock of truth shoots through him, afraid she might think he's talking about them.

And it *is* strange to be taking the decorations down when Christmas is just five days away. It doesn't feel like Christmas, even with the snow, and Deena's gift in his pocket. *He* doesn't feel like Christmas. He thinks of Bill Murray in *Scrooged,* how everything works out for him in the end, everyone from the TV station singing in front of the cameras, the chick from *Indiana Jones* kissing him, and Manny can't deny he'd like that. If one of the Powerball numbers hits, that's the only way it could happen, that last second miracle. Or maybe it already has. Maybe it was just everyone showing up, and everyone still being here. It's possible that he's missing the whole thing.

He scans the foyer for more decorations, but there's

only the marlin. What the hell are they going to do with it? What the hell would he do with it?

The lobsters aren't a mystery. They'll go to some other Lobster somewhere. They cost too much to chuck.

The bulbs and lights won't go anywhere though. He doesn't know who bought them, or when, but they don't belong to Darden Restaurants, Incorporated, any more than he does, and instead of stuffing them back in the storage closet, he flaps open a to-go bag and gently fits them inside, then sets the bag on the floor in the back hall directly under his jacket, as if daring anyone to call him a thief.

Jacquie and Roz are done in the dining room and head to the kitchen to take care of the coffee station. With the front buttoned up, Manny gets his End of Day running, and while it compiles, cleans out the cash drawer and prints the servers' reports from the bar's POS. He reconciles the piles of cash with their receipts, and while they had a terrible day (not worth stealing, he thinks), he's pleased to find they're off by less than two dollars. He counts the money three times before filling out a deposit slip and fitting it all in the pleather envelope, zipping it closed and locking it, then tucking it in the safe.

In back, the dishwasher's quiet. Rich is rolling away hot racks of water goblets, the casters leaving wet tracks. Leron is bagging the garbage, while in the big sink, steaming water drums into a mop bucket. Part of it's that they're closing early, but it seems to Manny that they're moving faster than they have all day.

"Okay," he says, to get their attention. "I need you guys to finish up, because in fourteen minutes"—he holds up the ticket—"we're all winning the Powerball. The only catch is that we have to share it with Eddie."

"Good luck," Roz says.

"The drawing's at exactly 10:59, in the bar. Drinks are on me."

"I can't believe you," Jacquie says, inspecting the ticket as if he got ripped off. "Why don't you just give us all a dollar?"

"Come on," Manny says, "you never know."

"I know you just threw away five dollars," she says, and now he really wants them to win—not the grand prize, just something.

Leron's bucket is almost full, and Manny wants to take a last look at the box behind the dumpster, so he volunteers to take out the garbage. The bag's extra heavy from all the food, the neck stretching as he duckwalks across the lot, afraid it will break on him. He opens the side door with a clang and muscles it up and in like a medicine ball, then stands there in the shadows, breathing hard, his hands cramped. The cold feels good. Against the fence, his footprints are the last ones—the box hasn't been touched. He flattens it and angles the cardboard through the side door, swings closed the chainlink gates, blocking them on the rebound, and locks the lock. Dom worked for him a long time, and while he understands he's not the only bartender who ever stole liquor, that's one letter of recommendation Manny wishes he could have back.

Leron never asked for one, and he's still here, mopping with Rich as the radio plays Jay-Z's "Hard Knock Life." With the dishwasher and the grill off, it seems too loud, but Manny doesn't say anything. He sneaks through the stockroom so he doesn't step on the wet floor. He pokes his head out the far end, checking the coffee station, then retrieves the three bottles, screening them with his body as he ducks into the back hall, and immediately bags them so no one will get the wrong idea. On the little ledge by the time clock he transfers the numbers from the Powerball ticket onto five Post-it notes, writing a name on each, all of them at random except one: He makes sure Jacquie's is Jacquie's.

According to the clock, they're seven minutes away from being rich.

"Just wet-mop it," he tells the guys, prompting an exaggerated double take. "And come out front when you're done. I've got a surprise for you."

Jacquie and Roz and Ty are already camped on stools, sipping frozen drinks and watching the UConn highlights. Manny slides behind the bar like he's going to serve them and sees that Jacquie has her diamond in.

"Whatcha got there?" Ty asks.

When he sets the bag down, the bottles clink. "Christmas bonus."

"Who for?"

"Who works the hardest around here?"

"You shouldn't have," Roz says, reaching.

"Sorry," Manny says, fending her off, "you got your bonus in your hand."

On the news they're showing one last look at the weather. The snow's supposed to stop before morning— perfect timing.

It's 10:55, then 10:56 as the anchors banter.

It's 10:57 when Leron and Rich saunter out of the break room. They look strange without their aprons, as if they've wandered in off the street. Manny presents them with their choice of the three bottles, setting them on the bar like prizes at a carnival. Leron laughs—"All right"—and shakes his head like it's a bad joke.

"I'm not going to tell you where I got them from. Let's just say the next time you see Dom you should thank him."

Leron lets Rich go first. He chooses the tequila. Leron picks the gin.

"Any takers?" he asks, showing the Hennessy to everyone. Finally Ty claims it.

"So," Manny says, "who's ready to win three hundred million dollars?"

"Gimme a minute," Roz says.

He makes a ceremony of dealing out the Post-its. The news is finally over, no credits, just the Fox copyright. Manny turns around to face the TV, thinking it doesn't have to be much, just a hundred bucks, or thirty-five, or five. Just a win to let them end the night right.

A middle-aged woman comes on, shilling for a local mattress store.

"Useless," Ty says.

Followed by a long commercial for a wireless carrier.

"This is stupid," Jacquie says. "You know what the odds are?"

"Thirty-six to one," Manny says. "Not the big prize, but to win anything."

They're going to love the new side dishes at Boston Market, the TV promises.

"Just show the fucking number," Ty says, as the cheap graphics for the drawing wash over the screen.

"It's the one and only Powerball," the announcer touts, "now bigger and better than ever! Hi everybody, Mike Pace here. That's right: three hundred and twenty-five million dollars is our jackpot tonight, that's the estimate, and more ways to win big with Powerball, including a chance to win a *billion* dollars with PowerPlay. Tonight's multiplier is two, number two will be the multiplier to-night—"

Already the balls are cycling like clothes in a dryer,

colliding, bouncing, dropping into a narrow plexiglass chute. The first one's going to be a 13.

"Crap," Rich says.

"That's just one," Manny says. "You don't have to get them all."

"Do you have to get them in order?" Roz asks.

"They put them in order from smallest to biggest," Manny says.

"So, no," Jacquie says.

"Check those tickets carefully," the announcer says. "There's 19, followed by 50—"

None of them have 50, Manny thinks, annoyed because they're going too fast. And forget 23.

"—and the last white ball is 41. Here we go, over three hundred million on the line, and the powerball is 13, 13 is—"

And like that it's over, and the guy is signing off, jabbering as fast as he did at the beginning.

"Well I got shut out," Roz says.

"I got a 19," Rich says.

"Damn," Ty says, crumpling his Post-it.

"How 'bout you?" Manny asks Jacquie. "Anything on yours?"

"No."

Leron just flicks his, sending it twirling down the bar.

"Hey," Manny says, "we tried. Hope Eddie had better luck than we did."

"Couldn'a done worse," Ty says.

"Hey," Roz says, "at least you got some booze out of the deal."

Manny turns the TVs off, not to break things up, but that's what happens.

"I'll take care of the drinks," he says, only Roz already has a tray, and he needs to turn off the sign by the highway, since it's past eleven.

While everyone else punches out, he closes back-to-front, by his checklist. For safety reasons, managers can't leave out the back, or alone. The kitchen floor is still drying, so he tries to step lightly, turning off the dishwasher and the radio, making sure the back door's closed. From habit he sniffs for gas as he passes the grill, quickly double-checks the reach-in and walk-in, then grabs the bag with the Christmas decorations and his lighthouse glass.

They're waiting for him in the break room—Ty wearing his slashed coat like Manny's twin, Leron fitting his skully over his ears precisely, as if it's a style. Manny remembers Jacquie going skating with him in that coat, the wispy fake fur of the hood tickling his chin, and burying his cold nose in her warm neck. She yelped and did the same to him, payback.

"Everybody got everything?" he asks.

"Looks like you got something," Roz says, and he opens the bag to show her.

"Only you."

"What is it?" Rich asks.

"Crap," she says.

They file out, Manny trailing, killing the lights. They stop at the front doors to bundle up while he clicks off the bar and then the dining room section by section until they're in the dark. Behind them the live tank burbles, while the wind whips snow over the walk. He cuts the outside lights, peering through the doors to be sure, then shoos everyone so he can set the alarm. On the wall, the marlin's curved belly glimmers, and he has to remind himself that this isn't his last time in the Lobster, even if it feels like it.

He does it quickly, not wanting to let Rich and Leron get away. They're already starting across the lot for the lights of the mall and the bus stop, and Manny has to chase after them, keys knocking at his hip, calling into the blizzard. They look back, wary, as if he might confiscate their bottles.

"Hey," he says, "I just wanted to thank you for working today," and shakes their hands. "If either of you guys is interested in the Olive Garden, come by this week and I'll see what I can do, 'cause Warren's definitely not getting it."

"All right," Leron says, or, "That's all right," Manny can't tell which.

"That's in Bristol," Rich asks.

"Think about it," Manny says, and lets them go.

Jacquie and Roz and Ty are trudging around the side, sticking to the tire tracks. The plow guy hasn't been back, and Manny wonders if he should call them, as if he's being graded on the lot tomorrow.

They all help Roz clean off her CRV. Manny clamps the end of his sleeve in his fingers and wipes off her headlights with his wrist. With her four-wheel drive she has no problem getting out of her spot, but waits for Ty and Manny, in case they need a tow. They don't, and Jacquie goes over to her window to say good-bye. It takes a while, a little powwow, and Manny wonders what they're talking about.

"See you Monday," Roz calls.

"Drive safe," Manny and Ty both say, waving her away.

It's time for good-byes, even though Rodney hasn't shown. Ty just assumes Manny will stay with Jacquie, and Manny's not going to argue.

"All right, boss," Ty says. He takes Manny's hand and draws him against his chest, thumping his back. He does the same with Jacquie, but gentler, bending to her, then gets in his Supra. "You kids have fun now."

"You know we will," Jacquie says.

Once he's gone, she gets in the Regal and tells Manny to pull around front. He has to put on a gangster lean to see around the patched window. He's so close to her he can smell the coconut of her lotion, and pictures her rubbing it in after a shower.

The wipers snag on the garbage bag. He stops them and cranks the defroster.

"I can give you a ride home if you want."

"Like this? No thanks."

"D'you call him?"

"He's like five minutes away."

Not much time, Manny thinks, but better than nothing.

They wait, facing the stop sign, snow slanting through his headlights, shifting with the wind like a spooked school of fish. The neon logo on the mall winks off, leaving an afterimage like a brand. Manny's doing his best not to smoke, when beside him Jacquie unzips a pocket inside her jacket and digs out a pack. By reflex he fishes for his lighter. When he flicks it, she's not holding a cigarette but a green velvet box, offering it to him like a gift.

So she'd planned this all along. And here he thought things were going his way for once.

He lets the light go out.

"Manny, I'm sorry, I can't keep this."

"It's yours."

"I know it is, and you know how much I love it, but I can't wear it when I'm with someone else. Do you understand that?"

"What am I going to do with it?"

"I don't know. I just can't keep it anymore, okay?"

She pushes the box toward him. If she dropped it now it would fall in his lap.

"Please, Manny? Don't make this harder for me."

She makes it sound like he's supposed to save her, doubly unfair, since she knows that's something he can't resist. In the dark he can't see the box, and imagines she's passing him a loaded gun. His hand closes around it, and it's his again, or no one's.

"Thank you," she says, and with a rustle of her jacket leans over and kisses his jaw up by his sideburn.

"Sure," Manny says, rubbing a thumb over the velvet.

"I probably got lipstick on you."

"That's okay."

"I was going to write you a letter, but I didn't think that was right."

"Thanks." But really, he wishes she'd be quiet. He looks beyond her to the road, expecting to find Rodney's headlights, but there's just another cop going somewhere.

"Hey, come on," she says, "we did the right thing. That's got to count for something."

"It's got to."

"Don't be like that."

"Like what?" he says, looking down.

"Like that."

The silence that follows reminds him of why they

broke up in the first place. At the end, he dreaded coming in when she was scheduled. The truce they declared was strange—not talking—but somehow easier than having the same fight day after day. He has the same headache now that he used to get from concentrating on their arguments, or maybe it's just the defroster drying out his sinuses.

He needs to change the mood, and remembers the two of them in her low bed, motionless and sated after making love, lying there as if asleep. That was the best time, even with the picture of Rodney in his cricket whites smiling down from the dresser. Silently he'd raise himself on one elbow to admire her, crane over and kiss her eyelids. It might seem like an illusion now, but he felt stronger then, smarter, thinner.

"You made me feel lucky," he says.

"Aw," she says, pressing a hand to her heart as if he's touched her. "You made me feel lucky too. If things were different with us . . ."

She seems content to let it rest there, and maybe that's as much of an explanation as he ever needed, he was just too stubborn to give up. He thinks he should ask if he can still call her, but knows the answer.

He could never figure out what to say to her. She was always a couple steps ahead of him. In some ways he liked the challenge of keeping up. Being with her sharpened him, and now, without her, he feels dull.

He watches a plow grind along the highway, its blade throwing a wake of snow. At the light, coming the other way, a long car pulls into the turning lane and waits, signaling.

"There he is," he says, and then, like a father's threat, "He better treat you right."

"I'm the one who needs to do better. You too. You want that baby to be proud of you."

"Yeah," he agrees mildly, unconvinced.

"You do."

The Caprice has turned in and is heading up the access road. For a second it's eclipsed by the giant mound of snow, then reappears, closer.

"Hey," he says, "thanks for coming in."

"What was I gonna do, say no? You know me better than that."

"You didn't have to stay." As he says it, he realizes he's waving the box at her, but she's watching Rodney make the left into the lot. His headlights pick out the cracks in Manny's windshield, silvering them for an instant.

"You gonna be okay?" Jacquie asks.

"Yeah," Manny says.

"You sure?"

"I'm sure."

Rodney's right beside them, their cars door-to-door like a drug deal.

"I've gotta go," she says, but hesitates, giving him a last look, as if that's a substitute for a kiss.

"Go," Manny says, and then when she opens the door, he ducks across the brake and waves to Rodney, who returns the wave like the good guy he is. He watches her walk around the hood and get in, hoping she'll look back, but isn't surprised when she doesn't.

Rodney glances over, giving him a chance to pull out first. Manny waves him on, as if he still has stuff to do here.

He doesn't have to stall long. He doesn't open the box, just adds it to the bag with his other souvenirs and sits there a minute, letting Rodney catch the light at the highway. He smooths the duct tape around the patch and adjusts the defroster—and remembers that he forgot to turn down the thermostat.

"Shit."

It would take him five seconds to slip in and reset the code. And now, with no one around and the Regal screening the front door, he wonders, nearly seriously, if he should steal the marlin. He can see himself driving away with the beak poking out a window. It's got to be held on with bolts, and he doesn't have the right tools. He can't just leave a big hole in the wall. Plus there's mall security circling the lots constantly. They're probably watching him, sitting here looking suspicious with his windshield busted in. The regular cops would probably think he's drunk. So no. The drive home's going to be a bitch as it is.

He reaches for his seat belt and discovers he's wearing it, shifts into drive and guides the Regal to the stop sign, signaling as if someone's behind him. The access road isn't bad, a wet path down the center. He's vaguely hungry, and thinks of the Wendy's on the far side of the mall, their spicy chicken sandwich and a cup of chili instead of fries. He knows it's open till midnight, but they might have closed with the snow. Not everyone's as crazy as he is.

At the light he has to decide, and finally takes a right, heading for Route 9 and home. He's fat enough, and it's been a long day already, with all the drama. It's late, and he needs to get to bed if he's going to make it in early tomorrow.

ACKNOWLEDGMENTS

Special thanks for sharing their inside knowledge goes to:
Jim Kehoe
Brynn Lafferty
Maria Lavendier
Esaul Rodriguez
Aaron Thompson

Constant thanks to my faithful readers:
Paul Cody
Lamar Herrin
Liz Holmes
Stephen King
Lowry Pei
Alice Pentz
Susan Straight
Luis Urrea

As always, deepest thanks to Trudy, Stephen, and Caitlin
for putting up with a year of Red Lobster talk.

And last, grateful thanks to David Gernert and Josh Kendall
for believing.